Little Red Hen

First published 1977 by Pluto Press Limited
Unit 10 Spencer Court, 7 Chalcot Road, London NW1 8LH

Tapes of the music for *Little Red Hen* can be
obtained through 7:84 Theatre Company (Scotland)
58 Queen Street, Edinburgh 2.

Pluto Press acknowledges the financial assistance of The Scottish Arts Council
in the publication of this volume and *Fish In The Sea*, also by John McGrath
and published simultaneously.

ISBN 0 904383 31 8

Designed by Tom Sullivan

Printed in Great Britain by Latimer Trend & Company Ltd Plymouth

John McGrath

Little Red Hen

Pluto  Plays

If you remove the English tomorrow, and hoist the green flag over Dublin Castle, unless you set about the organisation of the Socialist Republic, your efforts would be in vain. England would still rule you. She would rule you through her capitalists, through her landlords, through her financiers, through the whole array of commercial and industrialist institutions she has planted in this country.

James Connolly, 1897

Little Red Hen

7:84 Theatre Company was formed in 1971, with the aim of making theatre with socialist values for working-class audiences in England, Wales and Scotland. For the first two years we were based in London, and toured extensively, but in 1973 four of us who were Scots or had strong Scottish connections went off to start another company in Scotland, while the others carried on working in England and Wales.

The first production of the Scottish 7:84 was *The Cheviot, the Stag and the Black, Black Oil*, a show about the history of the Highlands. *Little Red Hen* was the sixth major production, which toured mostly in the industrial areas of Scotland from September to December 1975, also being performed subsequently in Ireland, and at the Shaw Theatre in London in June 1976.

Wherever we go in the industrial areas of Scotland – and Clydeside in particular – we meet up with an older generation of working-class militants who constantly astonish us. Active, articulate, passionate and well-informed, they draw their strength and conviction from the days of the 'Red Clyde' – days when the naked greed and ruthlessness of the capitalist system were plain to see; days when John Maclean, Jimmy Maxton, John Wheatley, Willie Gallacher and many other great activists and speakers expressed the demand of the Scottish working-class for the overthrow of capitalism and the creation of a socialist Scotland.

During the 1914–18 war, Glasgow was the centre of opposition to the senseless slaughter in the trenches, the exploitation of the workers in their factories to keep the slaughter going, and the rent-profiteers who owned their homes. After the war, in 1919, Glasgow workers lead the strike for a 40-hour working week to absorb the unemployed. There were 30,000 unemployed in Glasgow, and thousands more coming back from the trenches every week. On Bloody Friday, trouble flared up at a mass meeting in George Square. That night, the soldiers arrived and set up machine-guns on top of buildings in the city centre, and a howitzer in the City Chambers. The leaders were arrested. There was no violent revolution. But the anger, and the activism, continued. By 1922, the movement was so strong that ten out of the twelve Glasgow MPs returned at the election were socialists.

That generation saw Scotland on the move – in a big way. Today, we are told, Scotland is on the move again. The UCS work-in, the activism of the Scottish miners, the promised economic miracle of the oil industry, the upsurge of nationalism – all point to an atmosphere at least of energy and debate.

In *Little Red Hen*, we try to take a look at that earlier time of high hopes, and at the present moment of aspiration, through the eyes of one of that older generation. What went wrong with the first period – which ended in the misery of the '30s – may be of interest to people today who are working, as she did, for a better future for the people of Scotland.   J.McG.

List of characters:

Young Hen
Old Hen
Willie Gallacher
John Maclean
James Maxton
John Wheatley
Father (Freddie Mulrine)
Mother (Nora Mulrine)
George Mulrine
Charlie
Suave Young Man
J. Ramsay MacDonald
Lady Parmoor
Duchess Euphemia
Mrs Beatrice Webb
Labour MP's Wife
Davie Kirkwood
Sir F. Banbury
Deputy Speaker
General Thompson
King George V
Baldwin
Walter Citrine
Mrs Charlotte Square
Hamish Banff
William McCashin
Miner

LITTLE RED HEN by John McGrath
as presented by 7:84 Theatre Company (Scotland) in 1975

Dave Anderson	Composer/pianist; John Wheatley; Baldwin
Nadia Arthur	Costumes
Ginni Barlow*	Mother (Nora Mulrine); Mrs Beatrice Webb
John Bett†	James Maxton; Father (Freddie Mulrine); Suave Young Man
Wilma Duncan*	Young Hen
Feri Lean	Administrator; Publicity
Jennifer Lee†	Mother (Nora Mulrine); Mrs Beatrice Webb
John McGrath	Writer; Director
David Maclennan	Lighting design; Company Manager
Elizabeth Maclennan	Old Hen; Lady Parmoor; Accordion; Piano
Kris Misselbrook	General Thompson; Deputy Speaker; Stage Manager
Terry Neason	Singer; Caddy; Duchess Euphemia; Guitar
Bill Paterson	Harry Lauder; John Maclean; George Mulrine; J. Ramsay MacDonald
Bill Riddoch	Charlie; Willie Gallacher; Davie Kirkwood; Sir F. Banbury; Drums
Allan Ross	Set design and construction; Fiddle; Mandolin; King George V; Admiral Jelliroll
Ginni Stark†	Young Hen
Finlay Welsh*	James Maxton; Father (Freddie Mulrine); Suave Young Man
	with the help of:
John Byrne	Poster design and set painting
Pat Lovett	Choreography
	* first tour
	† second tour

A NOTE ON THE TEXT

While 7:84 Theatre Company work as a collective, we do not write plays in committee. We try to use the special skills of individuals within the company to their best advantage, while still laying the results of those skills open to discussion and criticism. *Little Red Hen* is, therefore, my creation as a writer, reinforced by the contribution of the members of the company in rehearsal and in discussion. Dave Anderson, as the main tune-writer, contributed to the lyrics of some of the songs. Elizabeth Maclennan not only did a great deal of research, but also gave much to the character of the Old Hen. Bill Paterson's knowledge of Glasgow, Bill Riddoch's knowledge of the North-east of Scotland contributed greatly to their parts, and David Maclennan's research and arguments greatly affect sections of the play. The whole company poured in their thoughts, knowledge and enthusiasm in a way that makes working with them a great joy.

J.McG.

ACT I

As audience comes in, one or two quiet tunes from the musicians.

On stage, four plinths, with fronts painted as the top of Greek columns, of varying height. As the show progresses these plinths are used for the politicians, and turn, flap, extend, etc., to become armchairs, cupboards, etc. – in fact all the scenery needed for the show. At the back of the stage, against a sky-cloth, a large, painted cut-out of Glasgow tenements. Where possible, this is flown out and a large cut-out of the Palace of Westminster flown in for the whole London sequence in Act One.

Suddenly, an OFFICIAL VOICE *comes over the speakers:*

Voice Clear the stage now, come on, boys and girls – (BAND *disperse, shruging.*) . . . Ladies and gentlemen – tonight, at your very own (*hall/club/theatre*) we are proud to bring to you – at immense cost to the taxpayer, no expenditure spared, not one penny of the Scottish Arts Council's budget languishing unlavished, ladies and gentlemen – you asked for it, you're going to get it – at long last Seven: Eighty-four Theatre Company presents – HARRY LAUDER!

Blast of accordion music, and mock HARRY LAUDER *appears, Och aye-ing, tells a few corny jokes and goes into a song. At chorus, all the* COMPANY *come on dressed identically as* HARRY LAUDER *and go through a Lauder routine of songs and dances, ending with 'Keep Right on to the End of the Road', then go, leaving the* YOUNG HEN *on stage. The overall impression is one of the old-style Tartan variety show, with yards of ersatz tartan, kilts, bonnets, etc., sentiment and joviality, climaxing in welter of emotion on the last number.*

TWO HENS

Young Hen Keep right on to the end of the road, eh? Aye, that's just what we're going to do, OK, keep right on to the end of the road until our own lovely Scotland's a nation once again: that's what I'm doing – and anybody who says any different should be dumped south of the border draped in a Union Jack, so they should. (*Sings*) Flower of Scotland, etc.

A disturbance. OLD HEN *waves her stick at her from audience.*

Old Hen Will yuh come down offa that platform and stop makin' a damn fool of yourself, Henrietta?

Young Hen Aw, Christ, it's ma Granny. See here, Granny, you go off and wave your red flag in Peking.

Old Hen Shut your ignorant face, you're a disgrace to your grandfaither – –

Young Hen What for? Jus' because I'm a patriot, a true Scot?

Old Hen Standin' there singing daft Harry Lauder songs, draped in yards of tartan like a Scottish Tourist Board rally – –

Young Hen Don't you say one word against Harry Lauder, Granny, he may have been a bourgeois pig, but he was loved – and for why? Because he made Scotland famous all over the world.

OLD HEN *is clambering up on to the stage. She is a thin, dynamic old lady with a stick, and a Glasgow accent that harks back a few years.*

Old Hen He made the Scottish people look damn stupid all over the world.

Young Hen (*To audience*) I really don't know what the older generation's coming to, I do not. She's always been like that – they old people should be seen and not heard, that's what I say – –

Old Hen Would you listen to that? Here's me been fighting for the labour movement in Scotland all my life, and her – the stupid baboon – tellin' me how she's gonnae make Scotland Free – –

Young Hen So we will – –

Old Hen Away and play wi' yoursel'.

Young Hen Granny! Would you no' be so obscene in front of these people? You're embarrassin' me.

Old Hen I don't give a damn for these people, I'm too far gone in my dotage to give a damn for anythin' but the truth.

Young Hen Aye, well. Could you just express it in a more kinda – acceptable manner?

Old Hen Away an' shite!

Young Hen You'll have to excuse her, she's gettin' past it – listen, Gran, I know you've had a fair scunner one way or another in your time, but we're not so stupid as you lot were – we know what we're doin'.

Old Hen Is that a fact?

Young Hen Aye! (*Sings*)

Oh Flower of Scotland,
When will we see,
Your like again . . .?

Old Hen Would you listen to her? Well I'm tellin' you, young woman, you're no' showin' a glimmer of doin' anything of the kind.

Young Hen When Scotland's free – we're gonnae say how it's run.

Old Hen D'you think?

Young Hen I know.

Old Hen You've more chance of Bonnie Prince Charlie comin' back from the grave to claim his rightful throne – when Scotland's free. There's two Scotlands, hen, and don't you forget it – there's the Scotland that's you and me, that's been robbed and cheated and worked to the bone when it suits or thrown on the queue at the burroo when it doesnae suit – that's one Scotland; and there's a Scotland that owns factories like yours and sweat-shops like I worked in, and grouse moors and mountains and islands and stocks and shares, and says what goes – and there's only one of them can be free at a time – and don't you go kiddin' yourself it's going to be the workers – –

Young Hen We're all gonnae be free.

Old Hen You know *nothin'*!

Young Hen Scotland's on the move, Gran – –

Old Hen Aye, but do you know which way you're goin'? Or how you're gonnae get there? Do you buggery – –

Young Hen Gran!

Old Hen I've seen something like it before, an' I'm for tellin' you about it – and listen tae what I'm tellin' you – for you'll need to remember – (STAGE MANAGER *comes on to remove tartan drapes.*) – Aye, you carry on, son, get rid of that rubbish – nineteen twenty-one. Scotland was on the move – and what was it we did then? Oh aye – it was the shimmy – Scotland, hen, was on the shimmy. (*Sings*)

> Aw Jimmy
> Come and dae the shimmy wimme
> Gimme a shimmy or two
> At the foxtrot I guess you're fine
> But Jimmy when you're wimme it's
> The shimmy for mine – ah luv it –
> Aw Jimmy
> Shake a shoulder, shake a shoulder
> Take a guid haud a me, do – o,
> Aw Jimmy when you're wimme,
> Aw heaven forgimme
> Ah could shimmy forever wi' you.

Do you like that?

Young Hen Does Hughie Green know about you?

Old Hen Oh there's worse to come. The whole place was doin' the shimmy – and I don't just mean in the dance-hall. The industrial proletariat of Scotland was on the march – and by God they had some great men to lead them – and they had the right ideas – Jimmy Maxton, John Maclean, John Wheatley, Willie Gallacher, Davie Kirkwood, Manny Shinwell – well – could they speak? You had to hear it to believe it – and you *did* go to hear it – thousands went to hear it: and the word they were speakin' was *socialism*. Not your wittery-wattery buggered-up capitalism with knobs on you get now – the real thing.

Come away and hear them at it –

LIGHT *comes up on* WILLIE GALLACHER *standing on plinth.*

Gallacher My name is Willie Gallacher from Paisley, and I've dedicated my whole life to the overthrow of capitalism. I've been an industrial militant ever since I started working for a rat of a greengrocer. I was Glasgow's first twelve-year-old shop-steward.

In nineteen nineteen I stowed on board a boat for Norway, and made my way to Moscow. When I met Lenin, he informed me I was too left-wing for him. So I was. All the same, he asked me to go back and help create the Communist Party of Great Britain – which I did. I believe there is only one way for the working people of this country to end the exploitation of their labour, and their lives, and that is to seize state power, retain it, and establish the dictatorship of the proletariat as a means of transition to a communist society. I will go to prison for believing that, I will suffer for it, but I shall die still firm to that belief and still working to bring it about.

Young Hen Hey, wait a minute, Gran, that fella's a communist.

Old Hen So he was. An' if you think he was a wee bit red, you wait till you hear this one.

LIGHT *comes up on* JOHN MACLEAN *on next plinth.*

Maclean My name is John Maclean from Pollokshaws. The monstrous war we have lived through shows that the day of social pottering or 'reform' is past. The 'social reformer' must be absolutely crushed, for intolerance to him is but justice to humanity. However Labour may attain power, it must do as the Bolsheviks are doing. It must get full possession of land and all means of production in order to use these co-operatively by the whole community for the advantage of all.

I stand four square for the ending of capitalism – in Scotland, as elsewhere in the world – and the establishment of the Scottish Workers Republic in which alone, we in Scotland can achieve true independence.

Young Hen That's the man that says what I say, good on you – what was his name?

Old Hen John Maclean.

LIGHT *goes up on* JAMES MAXTON.

Maxton My name is James Maxton, also from Pollokshaws. I'm a member of the ILP, I believe in Home Rule for Scotland, and I believe in socialism. Of course, for believing that, Calton Jail was for a spell my ancestral home. Labour must fight and fight to win! To win socialism in our time. The pathway of reformism or gradualism does not do for me when I see the children of Bridgeton going to school with a careworn look, when only joy and play should be in their minds.

It is all very well to say that we must build 'brick by brick' a structure of socialism – but you've got to get the bricks, and they are in the hands of capitalists. And even if you get the materials to build your edifice, you get it on capitalist conditions. In the end you find you have built not the Palace of Socialist Freedom, but a slum dwelling for the working classes.

We place our faith in the common working people of our land, inspired with courage, hope and determination, to build the new Society.

Old Hen Good old Jimmy – what a speaker, eh? You don't see the likes of that on your telly in between Robert Mackenzie and the bloody swingometer, do you my darlin'?

Young Hen Who's that one?

Light goes up on JOHN WHEATLEY.

Wheatley My name's John Wheatley, from Shettleston, and I'm a Pape; mind you, the Pope's no' very fond of me because I let it be known that I thought his encyclical on the rights of workers to respect private property and to do as they're told was a load of papal bull. I've stood on my own doorstep and watched two thousand drunk Catholics burning my effigy on the pavement. It was quite a good likeness.

I started my working life as a miner, ten years down the pit, then I got a job selling advertising space for the Catholic press. Then I had a great idea – free holy blotters, with a wee message from the clergy: and all around the edge – adverts. Valuable space. I cleaned up. Now I've got a small printing and publishing business of my own. Aye, well, it works out useful in the struggle. What's the struggle for?

A Labour majority in parliament to take over the land, take over the mines, establish socialism now, and end the criminal exploitation of man by his fellow man – that's what the struggle's for, and we are going to win. Don't be deceived by my diffident manner, comrades. I bloody mean it.

Old Hen That was the clever one, that Wheatley. He couldnae help being a Pape; but it did stop him gettin' to grips with Karl Marx, and that was his downfall.

Young Hen And was they all in the Labour Party?

All No we were not!

Gallacher Now when I met Lenin, he said to me – –

Maclean Don't listen to him – ever since he sneaked into the Kremlin he thinks he's Lenin's gramophone – seventy-eight revolutions per minute.

Gallacher Unfortunately my good friend Maclean here had went mental round about this time.

Maxton I have the greatest respect for these two gentlemen – mental or otherwise – but they tend to scare most people out of their wits, and if you're going to win an election, you need most people.

Wheatley There's enough to be done round here without arguing amongst ourselves. So let's get down off these soap-boxes and away and do something.

All Right.

They all go off, JOHN MACLEAN *alone,* WHEATLEY *and* GALLACHER *arguing,* JAMES MAXTON *whistling.*

Old Hen What a bunch! – and there was others, just as good. It was a great time to be alive and in Scotland. Apart from the poverty, the unemployment, the rickets, the TB and the beasts in the head.

Young Hen So which one of that crowd were you shouting for?

Old Hen Me? Oh, I couldn't give a damn about politics – till this particular night – I mind it well – it was just after tea time and there was five of us all squeezed into this room and kitchen. Ach, wait a minute – I'll show you. Make if you're me – (*Hands her a shawl and long skirt.*)

Young Hen Me? Be you? What do I dae?

Old Hen Get oot o' that daft Japanese tartan, and into these.

THE LOWER DEPTHS OF BRIDGETON

OLD HEN *goes up stage and yells to the company, who come on to listen.*

Old Hen Come on, you lot. Dae something for your living. Create – the Lower Depths of Bridgeton – well, shake a bloody leg.

As the COMPANY *set up the* MULRINE *family interior, a kitchen, with curtained bed recess and two armchairs, a sink and food shelves,* OLD HEN *talks to the audience.*

Old Hen They're supposed to be bloody actors, this lot, and they spend half their time singin' an' the other half drinkin'. I bet there's half of them no' paid up their Equity dues. (*To* COMPANY.) Now I want some proper actin', d'you hear? There's proper theatre-goers and theatre critics and God knows what else paid good money to see you, so none of your cheap satirical rubbish – d'you hear me? Are you right? (*Calls* FIDDLER.) Hey you, big fella, put down that can and set the mood with some suitable music . . . (FIDDLER *agrees, plays quiet tune.*)

Young Hen What do I do?

Old Hen Just sit down there, and think about fellas . . .

Young Hen Big fellas, little fellas, or what?

Old Hen Suit yoursel'. They're a' the same whatever shape they come in. Now here's your brother George. He was in the war, was George, and now he doesnae say anything.

Young Hen Nothin' at all?

Old Hen Well, he's no just a dummy, you know, but he was awf'y quiet. He's makin' a jumpin' jack for your wee sister Agnes. There's your mother worrying herself stupid about Agnes – so were we all. And – oh God, here's your faither comin' and he's got somebody wi' him.

Gestures to FIDDLER *to desist, which he does quietly. She watches as* FATHER *and* CHARLIE *come on, arguing about football. They come to the door.*

Father Will you no' come in for a wee minute, Charlie?

Charlie No – no – no, I'll go on up the stairs – I'm taking round these wee pamphlets for the election, you know – here, there's one for you, see an' you come to the meetin'. I'll distribute these to the folk up the stair.

Father What's this for?

Charlie It's tellin' you to get out and vote for Jimmy Maxton, which I hope you do anyway, and it's tellin' you there's a few meetings you should be getting along to, right?

Father Meeting? Votin'? Here, take it, don't waste your good pamphlet on me – I don't vote. Nor do I go to meetings.

Charlie How no'?

Father It's no' for the likes of me.

Charlie That's just who it *is* for – the likes of you and the likes of me. Christ, if you've never even voted, it's about time you did – –

Father (*Awkward*) No, no – no, no.

Charlie Well just read it, won't you, Freddie, it's for you.

Father Well, I'll take one in wi' me, eh?

Charlie See that – 'Housing: We in the ILP refuse to accept the appalling conditions in which the working class is forced to live. Here in Bridgeton alone . . .'

Father Charlie – can you no' see? I cannae read.

Charlie Oh. Well – that's nothin' to be ashamed of, Freddie. Here – is that how you've never voted?

Father Aye. I wouldnae know what to do. But I'll give one to the girl – she likes readin'.

Charlie Do you want to vote?

Father Well, I suppose I should.

Charlie And if you did – who'd you vote for?

Father Well it'd no' be the Tory, I'm no' that stupid.

Charlie And Nora?

Father Och, she's worrit senseless wi' the wain, she'll no' be wantin' to go votin' or nothing like that.

Charlie And what about George?

Father No. He'll no' shift. It's three years since he came back, but the war's just finished him off. He's no' daft or shell-shocked or anythin' – but he'll no' vote. It's too much like speakin'.

Charlie Maybe I will come in then for a wee minute . . .

Father Will ye? Aye. Come on then, son.

They go in to the small area of the room. GEORGE *gets his jumping jack to work, and shows it proudly.*

Mother Oh, here, that's great. (*To* AGNES, *who is behind curtains.*) Here, Agnes, see what George's made for you – look at it, is it no' good? (*To* FATHER.) Aw God, Freddie, she'll no' even raise her eyes to look at it, poor wee thing.

Father Is she no' better?

Mother Well, I wouldnae say she's worse, but she's no' exactly better – it's this bloody room, the walls is wringing wet and she cannae get air to breathe at all. (*To* CHARLIE.) Hello, Charlie.

Charlie Aye, Nora. I'm sorry about the wain.

Mother She's no' right.

Father Here, girl – (*To* YOUNG HEN.) – somethin' tae read.

Young Hen Oh – what is it?

Father Meeting – votin': Charlie's – er . . .

Charlie Look, I'm sorry to bother you at a time like this wi' sickness in the family, but I'm bound to say, I find it incredible that wi' the situation you're in, there's not one of you going out to vote for the one man who's likely to try an' make things better for you.

Young Hen Jimmy Maxton, do you mean?

Charlie I do, hen. There's folk fightin' in the trade unions for better wages for us and decent hours and better conditions and you're supportin' *them* I hope . . . no?

Father They trade unions is trouble.

Charlie You'll no' get anything without a bit of trouble, Freddie. But what we need now is Maxton and his colleagues to get up there into parliament an' tell them fools in London we're no' standin' for it any more.

Silence.

Look, missus, you've said it yourself. These old houses are no' fit to be lived in the way they are – no wonder yer bairn's sick, no wonder she's no' gettin' better – now I'm not sayin' 'Get out and vote for Maxton and you're gonnae get three months' holiday on the French Riviera', no, but what I am saying is if us and the likes of us don't vote for him and the likes of him, this tenement's still going to be standing here in fifty years' time, still wringin' wet, still stuffed full of sick bairns and under-paid, overworked people. For why? Because the place is owned by a landlord – right? Now what does that mean . . .?

He carries on as OLD HEN *speaks over.*

Old Hen Could that boy argue? He made George Bernard Shaw sound like Basil Brush. I sat mesmerised: a whole new side of life I'd never even knew existed – and a whole new side of Charlie Sullivan I'd never even knew existed.

Father See, Charlie, old Fairlie that owns this house – right? Well – he's paid for it. Out of his own money. So it's *his*. Right? Am I right or am I wrong?

Charlie Oh, God, Freddie, you're under the thumb of the system.

Father Oh – wait a minute – no – I'm wrong. Now Charlie's gonnae tell me where I'm wrong. Fella buys somethin' out his own pocket – but it's no' *his*. Come on now, Charlie, tell me where I've gone wrong.

Charlie Right, well – whose house are we in now – yours or mine?

Father Mine – no – his. Like – I'm livin' in it, but it's his. If he doesnae want me livin' in it – oot. He throws me oot. That's the story.

Charlie Right. Now I go and buy a knife, a very sharp knife – I pay for it out of my own money, out of my own pocket – so it's mine. And I think – that's a good wee knife that, I wonder if it would cut a finger off. So I go in the pub – go up to somebody – a total stranger – and I cut his finger off. What's wrong wi' that?

Father It's no' your finger.

Charlie No, but it's my knife. And if your landlord can throw you out because it's his house, how can I no' cut your finger off with my knife? It's no my finger – but it's no' the landlord's wife and wains'd be on the street: that man'll be doin' you a hell of a sight more actual grievous bodily harm throwin' you on the street than I would be cutting your finger off, but what he does is legal – sanctified in the law of the land. Well, that law's gonnae change – when Jimmy Maxton gets enough votes.

Mother (*Comes in from bed recess, worried.*) Here, I'm away to get the doctor: that wain's no gonnae last till mornin' . . . I think you'd better have your argument somewhere else . . .

Charlie Oh, I'm sorry, Nora – am I disturbing her?

Mother That's alright, Charlie. If what you say is right, Charlie, and this man's gonnae speak up for us, you're quite right to do what you're doin'. But he's no' gonnae be in time to help that one. It's a doctor she's needing, no' a politician. (*She goes out.*)

Charlie I'll go.

Father Maybe you'd better, Charlie. (*As* CHARLIE *goes,* FATHER *stops him.*) Er . . . I'll vote for the man.

Charlie Right. Cheerio. I hope – aye, well. (*Goes.*)

Silence.

Father Well, George?

George (*Clears his throat uneasily.*) They're a' the same.

Father Oh Christ. Charlie's away an' left his wee pamphlets . . .

Young Hen (*To* OLD HEN.) What do I do now?

Old Hen Put on your skates and deliver the bloody things tae every house in the close and every close in the street – that's what you do . . .

MUSIC *in, as* YOUNG HEN *takes pamphlets and goes.*

Old Hen That was the day I joined the ILP.

SINGER *sings 'Red Hen' song:*

Little hen goes running round
From street to street
Doing what there is to do –

Little hen goes running round
She's found her feet

Nothing's going to stop her
Till the job is through . . .

MUSIC *continues*.

Old Hen (*Speaks over.*) Christ, did I work – well, the job was there to be done, and a' my life – if there was something needin' daein', I'd just get up an' dae it – pamphlets? Leaflets? I've delivered millions of them from that day to this; chalking out the streets for the speakers, putting out the chairs in the halls, sweeping the bloody halls, makin' the tea, addressin' envelopes, shifting jumble: well, I was nae good at arguin' or speakin' – but that was what I could dae, so I did it. (*Song up again.*)

Planting little seeds to grow one day
Grow up into fields of wheat
Little Red Hen, like the story books say
Works so one day we can eat.
Little hen gives all her strength
To win that fight
Seems her strength is never done
Little hen gives all she has
She knows she's right
Nothing's going to stop her
Till the fight is won.

During the last part of the song, YOUNG HEN *goes back into the room, in her character as the* YOUNG OLD HEN, *worn out.* CHARLIE *comes in, and persuades her to set off again with more pamphlets. As the song ends she comes back on to* OLD HEN *as herself.*

VICTORY, AND OFF TO WESTMINSTER

Young Hen Did yous win?

Old Hen We battered them – They Tories in the Western Club must have thought the world had come to a full stop. Out of twelve seats in Glasgow – the ILP won ten. Fair enough, the Tories won the election, but we won Glasgow. Nineteen twenty-two was the year the Red Clyde reached its parliamentary apotheosis – –

Young Hen You what?

Old Hen And demonstrations? Aw, you missed yoursel' – you bourgeois nationalists thought you had a bit of a send-off for Winnie Ewing when she got in – eh?

Young Hen Aye, it was great – I was there.

Old Hen Nuthin'. St Andrews Halls were packed to the rafters the night before they went. They pledged theirselves to do God knows what; we sang the Hundred and Twenty-fourth Psalm, we sang the Twenty-third Psalm, Neil Maclean announced the old parliamentary order was finished, Manny Shinwell was wondering just how they could possibly live up to it all, and Jimmy Maxton got up to speak. There was silence.

(*During this speech the room set is transformed back into plinths.*)

Young Hen Did he forget his speech?
Old Hen Shut up! You wee besom.

MAXTON *gets up on to a plinth.*

Maxton Comrades and friends: We who are going off to Westminster do not go as so many individuals to win glory for ourselves. We go as a team – a team working towards one goal – and that goal is the abolition of poverty. There is some talk – there are some people talking – in a worried kind of a way – about the 'atmosphere' of the House of Commons getting the better of us wild men from the Clyde. Comrades – I've got news for them: the atmosphere of the Clyde is going to get the better of the House of Commons.

CROWD *sing 23rd Psalm.*

Old Hen And there was such a shout and cheers and the next night there was at least one hundred thousand people in St Enoch Square to see them off – where's your Winnie Ewing the noo?

In background, 'Red Flag' takes over from 23rd Psalm. WHEATLEY, *with overcoat and case, comes on.*

Wheatley Until this day, in my practical politics as a Baillie and a member of the Glasgow Corporation, I have been a cautious man. I have acted on the principle that we, as socialists, must not go too far ahead of what the mass of the people want. When I see these streets lined with people, when I see the square in front of the station jammed tight with over one hundred thousand citizens madly enthusiastic, not for the MPs themselves, but for the socialism for which they stood, I know I was wrong. It is being proven to me, at this minute, beyond doubt, that the people are ready to respond to a bold socialist lead.

'*Red Flag*' *ends.*

Young Hen So: what happened?
Old Hen So what happened – they got on the train.

MAXTON *and* WHEATLEY, *with their suitcases, get on to the train – two stools side by side facing the audience. The* BAND *starts a slow train rhythm, that speeds up as* MAXTON *and* WHEATLEY, *excited and determined, sit discussing what they are going to have to do at Westminster. As the rhythm works up to full speed,* WHEATLEY *jumps up and starts to sing a mock 'tough' number –*

Wheatley 'We're gonna shake Westminster
till its bells start to ring –
Gonna make a hell of a noise –'

Maxton jumps up and joins in:

Maxton/Wheatley (*Together*)
    Gonna make them sorry that they started this thing –
Wheatley Right, Jim?
Maxton Right, boys –
Wheatley 'We're gonna raise the Red Flag over
        Ten Downing Street,
    Gonna throw King George on the burroo' –
Maxton/Wheatley (*Together*)
    Gonna agitate until the Soviets meet –
Wheatley Right, Jim?
Maxton Too true–

> SINGERS *join in as the* BAND *gets up steam – and* MAXTON *and* WHEATLEY *sleep uncomfortably.*

Singers Night-train –
    Through the unknown places
    Leaving –
    What they knew,
    Far from –
    Those familiar faces –
Maxton/Wheatley (*Jumping up from sleep.*) Do we have to change our train at Crewe?
Singers Cruising
    Through the English Country
    Things go –
    Bump in the night
    Strange sounds
    On the English platform –
Wheatley Wake, Jim?
Maxton Too right . . .

> *Train starts to slow down.*

Wheatley Feeling kind of homesick and we haven't arrived
    Feeling kind of tired and low –
Wheatley/Maxton (*Together*)
    Feeling unconnected wanting back to the Clyde –
Singers Euston!
Maxton/Wheatley (*Together*)
    Euston?
Singers Euston!
Maxton/Wheatley (*Together*)
    Oh no . . .

> MAXTON *and* WHEATLEY *doze off again. The skyline of Glasgow drops down and the Houses of Parliament arise in sunny splendour.*

A figure in frock-coat appears tentatively behind them: J. RAMSAY MAC-
DONALD. *He looks at them, and then addresses the audience over their
heads, in rhyming couplets, with occasional asides in prose.*

MacDonald J. Ramsay MacDonald speaking
    A great parliamentary career's what I'm seeking:
    I may look like a bit of a smarty
    But in fact I'm in the Labour Party.

    When they say that my politics are soft
    I remind them – I was born in a croft
    And though I now hob-nob with grand lords
    I once fearlessly criticised the landlords.

(*Confidentially*) In a preface to a book, as a matter of fact; of course
that was in nineteen hundred and five, and some long time ago, but a little
reputation for being red goes quite a long way in the Labour Party;
damned useful, too.

    Now this man Clynes is a boring wee bleeder
    It's time *I'd* a shot at being Labour leader –
    But alas and alack, woe betide!
    I'm in need of the votes of these wild men from the Clyde –
    I'll stand in a good left-wing stance (*Poses*)
    Then maybe I'll stand a bit of a chance –

    So watch this: I think you'll be impressed –

(*To* MAXTON *and* WHEATLEY, *using mock Glasgow accent.*) Hullo rare
Jimmies, we's – eh – ah – we's are gonnae have a wee bit vote an' that,
for leader, if ya follow me, boys – see what I mean – it's like, well, see that
fella Clynes – well – it's either him or me. So who're you voting for?

Maxton Clynes?
Wheatley Or you?
Maxton/Wheatley (*Together*) We abstain.
MacDonald Oh, come on now – don't forget, I'm your boy – I'm dead Red.
    I am a big wheel in the ILP –
    Surely you boys are going to vote for me?
Maxton/Wheatley (*Together*) We'll think about it . . .
MacDonald Good –
    Then at this point I will be gone.
    You'll be seeing more of me anon.
(*Pauses*) I'm going to exit left. I think that's significant. Of course, it
won't look left to you. It'll actually look right to you. But if it looks right
to you, I'm satisfied.

He goes. WHEATLEY *looks at* MAXTON.

Maxton Clynes or MacDonald? John – what have we done?
Wheatley We have joined his Majesty's loyal Opposition . . .

They pick up their cases and go. MUSIC *immediately begins, and the set changes to smart London interior – a party given by wealthy Labour supporters.*

COCKTAILS

GENERAL THOMPSON, ADMIRAL JELLIROLL, LADY PARMOOR, DUCHESS EUPHEMIA, J. RAMSAY MACDONALD, MRS BEATRICE WEBB, SUAVE YOUNG MAN *and* THE HON. DOUGALL *come on with drinks.*

Suave Young Man (*Comes and chatters excitedly to the audience.*) We think they're going to be awfully droll – haven't you heard? They're going to be fascinating – in an appalling sort of way: we're getting fifty-six brand new Labour MPs – all to ourselves – one simply can't wait. Lancashire lads, doubtless in clogs, with all the latest scandals from Heckmondwyke – what a laugh: tiny Welsh miners with their Davy lamps to lighten our darkness; the girls are agog, one hears; gruff Yorkshire terriers, chattering tales of muck and brass; in Bradford – I think that's in Yorkshire; and the Scotties, oh, there's a thrill, in *kilts*, with *claymores*, skirling away on their bagpipes – muttering strange incomprehensible sounds about Lenin, and bloody revolution. And all of them, all of them – well, nearly all of them – breathing fire – one simply longs to see them.

At the end of song, J. RAMSAY MACDONALD *breaks away and, as music continues languidly on piano:*

MacDonald All those wild men roaring down from the Clyde
        And Wales and the North and God knows where beside
        Are turning my party into a fearsome scrimmage
        They're common, uncouth and spoiling our image.

        For Government's high office we must seem to be fit –
        But how can that be when they belch and scratch and spit
        The people who matter will soon make a mockery
        Of their Welshity, Northernness and unspeakable Jockery

        Now I'm the leader I shall make it my job
        To teach them good manners, to curtsey and bob
        A party of workers is obviously rejectable
        I shall make it my business to make them eminently respectable.

As J. RAMSAY MACDONALD *ends*, ALL *advance on audience and sing.*

All   Going to Westminster's rip-ping fun
        Now you've won
        It's better than Shettleston
        But for a chap to get on a bit
        One must take one's cocktails –

LADY PARMOOR *goes over and accosts* WHEATLEY.

Lady Parmoor Ah, Mr Wheatley . . .

Wheatley Yes, Lady Parmoor, what can I do for you?

Lady Parmoor I find it distressing that so far as I know I have not had the pleasure of meeting *Mrs* Wheatley – I was asking myself whether she might no care to drop in on one of my Tuesday luncheon parties? She'd meet some frightfully keen people . . .

Wheatley Mrs Wheatley prefers to live in Glasgow.

Lady Parmoor Oh, Oh, how amusing . . .

Wheatley And besides, Tuesdays is wash day.

MUSIC *up*. LADY PARMOOR *goes off, laughing wildly*. ALL *sing*.

All   Living in London is Oh So Sweet
        Quite a treat
        It's better than Rutherglen
        But to be wholly acceptable
        One must have good manners.

MUSIC *goes on*, DUCHESS EUPHEMIA *chats to* MRS BEATRICE WEBB.

Duchess Euphemia My dear, d'you know the other day I was fascinated to read that the wife of your Deputy Leader – what's his name? Sounded Jewish – ah yes, Clynes – that Mrs Clynes believes the time is ripe for the daughters of Labour leaders to be presented at Court – whatever next – socialist debutantes . . .

Mrs Beatrice Webb And why not, pray – there's nothing inferior about socialists . . .

Duchess Euphemia The season will never be the same – lawks a mussy – champagne and pigs' trotters . . .

MUSIC *comes up as* ALL *sing next bit of song*.

All   Be a sport and join in the game
        Life's too short, too boring and tame
        Don't be liverish and so working-class
        Speak our gibberish, or you'll end up on your arse –

        – Ha ha-ha, Ha ha-ha –

        Going to Westminster's rip-ping fun
        Now you've won
        It's better than Dennistoun
        But for a chap to get on a bit
        One must show good breeding.

A LANCASHIRE LABOUR MP'S WIFE *appears, smiling coyly. She commits a social blunder, then is lead forward:*

Labour MP's Wife I have lived all my life among the cotton mills of Lancashire. Now my husband is in parliament, I can safely say I have achieved

my life's ambition. I have met Her Majesty the Queen. And she is a Very
Gracious Person.

MUSIC *swells up*. WHEATLEY, MAXTON *and* KIRKWOOD *walk into the party –
squeals of delight, etc.* ALL *sing except them.*

All   What a treat, some Labour MPs
They're so sweet, so easy to please
Though they may be rough, they're the craze today
When we've had enough, we can send them all away.

MUSIC *continues as* KIRKWOOD *speaks to a circle.*

Kirkwood See, ah'd just got up and made this speech, about the desperate
conditions of the crofters in the Outer Hebrides. The Tories listened in
silence – then voted to do nothing about it. As I was leaving the House of
Commons, this Tory MP comes up to me – Mr Kirkwood? he says. Aye,
Davie Kirkwood here. Mr Kirkwood, I could not vote for you but I
should like to help these people if I may. Here – take this five pound note.

WHEATLEY *and* MAXTON *exchange glances and go away from group in
general direction of the piano.* KIRKWOOD *is buttonholed by* MRS BEATRICE
WEBB.

Mrs Beatrice Webb Tell me, Mr Kirkwood, what do you think of our parliament?

Kirkwood Well, to speak the truth to you, Mrs Webb – or should I not say
Lady Pasfield?

Mrs Beatrice Webb No, no. We're Fabians, we don't use the title: call me
Beatrice.

Kirkwood That's just an example of what I was going to say: before I entered
the House of Commons, I'm afraid I knew little of the Great Ones, the
Powerful Ones, the Lordly Ones; by the way, you can read all this in
my autobiography – *My Life of Revolt* – but when I entered the House
I found it was full of wonder. I had to shake myself occasionally as I
found myself walking about and talking with men whose names were
household words. More strange was it to find them all so simple, un-
affected and friendly.

Sighs of relief and content all round, as tune comes in again. ALL *sing.*

All   The life of a gentleman's frightfully nice
Don't think twice
It's better than navvying –
Kirkwood (*Solo.*) Choose the right friends, in a year or two –
You can join the peerage
All   Be a sport and join in the game
Life's too short, too boring and tame
Don't be liverish and so working-class
Speak our gibberish or you'll end up on your arse.

Going to Westminster's awful fun
Now you've won
It's better than Shettleston
But for a chap to get on a bit
One must take one's cocktails.

ALL *sweep off laughing and braying with confidence.*

HARD WORDS AT WESTMINSTER

Enter YOUNG HEN *and* OLD HEN, *dismantling cocktail party set.*

Young Hen There y'are, you see – jus' what do you expect? Let decent, honest people go down to London and they'll turn into monkeys on sticks. What I say is – they should have stayed here where we can keep an eye on them.

Old Hen Ye're talking rubbish – you couldnae even keep an eye on the Glasgow Corporation – and that's just up the street.

Young Hen It's no' rubbish. That's why I say we should have our own parliament, right here in Scotland.

Old Hen Aye, but don't you see, hen, it's no' so simple – it was the bourgeois parliament itself that buggered them up. Listen to that David Kirkwood, him that was working at Parkhead Forge wi' the arse out of his breeks – 'how strange to find them all so bloody friendly'. Naw, it was no' so strange, Davie. They were after you, boy, they needed you, and by Christ they got you.

Young Hen And did they all end up like him?

Old Hen No, hen. Jimmy Maxton and John Wheatley took a fair scunner to the whole Westminster wonderland, and Maxton thought he was going to get a hold of the House of Commons and shake it till its bells rang – give him his due – he went at it like he said he would.

Scene is changing to House of Commons. On comes DEPUTY SPEAKER, MAXTON, WHEATLEY, SIR F. BANBURY, *etc.*

It was this hot June afternoon. Our parliament was discussing public health in Scotland – *viz*, they were taking away the milk from sick babies. Some Tory doctor MP from Dumfries arose to say how people didnae need health anyway. There was a couple of Tories too geriatric to move out, and a few of the Clyde men were waiting and watching. At six o'clock Jimmy got up to speak to a deserted House.

Maxton I have listened to the speeches of the Under Secretary of State and of the Hon. Member for Dumfries with some considerable impatience, because I feel that both of them have been doing their very best to soothe the public conscience on a matter in regard to which the public conscience has no right to be at ease.

I gather from the report that in Scotland last year there were twelve thousand, four hundred and seventy-two cases of tuberculosis notified.

There is some division of opinion as to the causes of this disease; there is much division of opinion as to treatment and possibilities of cure: but it is admitted by all that sunlight is an important element; and that good, nutritious, wholesome food is also an element, both in preventing the disease and in effecting a cure.

In another part of the Report, we find the statistic dealing with the poorhouses of Scotland. To maintain an average man, his wife and four children in the Barnhill Poorhouse costs fifty-eight and sevenpence ha'penny per week. In the City of Glasgow there are few skilled artisans *getting* fifty-eight and sevenpence ha'penny a week, and the unskilled and semi-skilled labourers in my constituency get something like thirty-two and sixpence per week.

For this reason, not only are they denied food, clothing and house accommodation, but even the free gifts of God: sunshine and fresh air, for fresh air and sunlight cannot be got in a big proportion of our tenement dwellings.

That seems to me to be a very definite and clear indication as to where the breeding-ground for some of your tuberculosis is to be found, at least. And I am surprised that the Hon. and gallant gentleman gets up as a politician and attempts to defend a state of things which as a medical man would receive his wholesale condemnation.

We have the definite statement in the report: 'We have continued to carry out a policy of rigorous economy because we must save money.'

Sir F. Banbury Hear, hear.

Maxton A right Hon. gentleman on the other side said hear, hear to the idea of saving money. It was the Right Hon. Baronet, the Member for the City of London.

Sir F. Banbury I am ready to answer anything.

Maxton I do not think there is an answer to your remark. Last year the number of children in Scotland who died in their first year rose to eleven thousand, six hundred and sixty-four. That is one thousand, two hundred and sixty-five children *more* than in nineteen twenty-one. One thousand, two hundred and sixty-five children who would have lived in nineteen twenty-one.

The Hon. and gallant gentleman says the withdrawal of milk and food supplies from the mother had no effect that is reflected in the statistics. Does he mean to tell me as a medical man that the withdrawal of milk from a baby gives it a better chance of life?

In the course of his professional career, the Hon. Member for Dumfries must have seen thousands of infants under one year suffering, and he must have seen the parents watching over the little one hovering between life and death.

I only saw one case and that made a mark on me that I shall never lose. I saw a mother struggling with the last ounce of her energy to save the life of an infant and in saving it she lost her own. I am not interested in the statistics of this. I am interested in the tens of thousands of fathers and mothers tonight who are watching over their babies, wondering whether they are going to live or die. If I can strike the public conscience to see that this is absolutely wrong and unjustifiable in a Christian nation, I should think I had rendered some service to my country.

The circular letter reversing the supply of milk and food was issued on the twelfth of March nineteen twenty-two, when the death rate was at a higher point than it had been for many years, due to an epidemic of measles, influenza and whooping-cough. In the same circular letter, the Scottish Health Board intimated it would no longer approve of the provision of hospital accommodation for children suffering from whooping-cough and measles. At a time when an epidemic was raging, these Hon. Gentlemen on the other side of the House, in the interests of saving money, which the Right Hon. Baronet the Member for the City of London approves of, condemned children to remain in the breeding-ground of infection. In the interests of economy they condemned hundreds of children to death, and I call it *murder*! I call the men who initiated the policy murderers. They have blood on their hands – the blood of infants. It is a fearful thing for any man to have on his soul – a cold, callous, deliberate crime in order to save money.

We are prepared to destroy children in the great interest of dividends. We put children out in the front of the fighting-line – –

Sir F. Banbury On a point of order – –

Maxton I will not give way. Not for one moment. You are one of the worst in the whole House!

Hon. Members Sit down!

Maxton I certainly will not sit down!

Deputy Speaker The Right Hon. Baronet is raising a point of order.

Sir F. Banbury Is it in order for an Hon. Member to call other Hon. Members 'murderers'?

Hon. Members It's true! He's proved it!

Deputy Speaker I do not think it is in order for the Hon. Member to use that term.

Maxton If the Hon. Baronet will supply me with a word that describes his action, other than that of 'murderer', I will use it. Failing that, I stick to what I have said.

Sir F. Banbury On a point of order – –

Deputy Speaker (*To* MAXTON.) I have already said that to call any Hon. Member of this House by that name is not in order.

Maxton There is only one word that applies, and I applied it to all Members who supported the initiation of this policy, and I applied it particularly to the Right Hon. Baronet, the Member for the City of London – –

Sir F. Banbury On a point of order – –

Deputy Speaker I hope the Hon. Gentleman will withdraw the remark as applying to any particular Member of this House.

Maxton I can never withdraw. I did it deliberately.

Old Hen And do you know what happened? They 'suspended' him – threw him out: no *him*, the child murderer – no – it was: Jimmy Maxton, you are guilty of telling the truth in the House of Commons – OUT. (MAXTON *gets up and walks deliberately out of the House of Commons. Followed later by* WHEATLEY.) And Wheatley got up and he said they were murderers, too, and bugger them: it was John Wheatley – OUT.

So Maxton and Wheatley was planning this big campaign all over England and Wales and Scotland to get themselves support – when canny wee Ramsay stepped in . . .

A CUNNING RUSE

J. RAMSAY MACDONALD *peeps out from behind the Speaker's Chair.*

MacDonald I might have known we'd have trouble sooner or later.
And one of those wild men would be the instigator.
We must have good manners, dignity, sweet reason.
These damn'd Glasgow keelies are guilty of treason –

And now they're proposing to storm through the land
Attacking our democracy, red flag in hand;
Mocking our parliament, rousing the rabble
Frightening the voters and stirring up trouble.

If they lose then we all lose, our party is dead
If they win then I'm done for – they'll chop off my head.

Now nothing in my view could possibly be more sinister
So I've conspired and colluded with the Tory Prime Minister
Democracy will be served, parliament will win
They're too dangerous to be out, so we'll let them back in.

When they're least expecting it – ssh!

WILLIE GALLACHER *enters as* J. RAMSAY MACDONALD *goes out.*

Gallacher Willie Gallacher here again, folks. By now I'm down in London, too – I tried to get into parliament as a Communist for Dundee, but they wouldnae have me so I'm down here working as a journalist on the Party newspaper. I picked up a highly confidential whisper in the House of Commons they were gonnae lift the suspension, so I dashed round to my friend John Wheatley and told him.

JOHN WHEATLEY *in his hotel room.* GALLACHER *walks in.*

Wheatley Is that a fact? Now that's a bloody nuisance – I've got a whole campaign organised on the basis of being slung out. How dare they let us in?

Gallacher Well, if you'll take my advice, you'll publicly demand to be re-instated.

Wheatley What?

Gallacher Your constituents have been unrepresented at Westminster for too long.

Wheatley Aye, about two hundred and fourteen years. What are you driving at?

Gallacher Look: go down publicly to Westminster and try to *force* your way in – just ten minutes before they unexpectedly decide to open the doors to you . . .

Wheatley I begin to cotton on – so that way . . .

Gallacher It will look as if they've given in to your demands . . .

Wheatley William, you're wasted on the Communist Party – you should have been a Tory Chancellor of the Exchequer.

Gallacher I'm working on it. Do you agree?

Wheatley I'll consult my colleagues.

Gallacher (*To audience.*) And that's just what they did. Jimmy Maxton goes up to the front door saying let me in, in the name of the people of Bridgeton – the poor constable says I'm sorry in you cannae go – and all the newspapermen is there enjoying the panto, when, right on cue, out rushes the other lads waving their arms – You've won, lads, you've won – the British Parliament has lifted your suspension – what a Mighty Victory! (*Goes*)

Old Hen Away, Willie Gallacher, you're gey clever, but you're a damn fool.

Young Hen What? That was a rare idea.

Old Hen The day they boys were sucked back into the Westminster whirlpool was a black day for every worker in Scotland – aye, and in England, too. If they'd told that lot of bourgeois bum-lickers to stuff their parliament up their backsides, they might have saved the Labour movement. If they'd gone off to the workers and the ordinary party members and organised a rebellion against MacDonald and his tomfoolery, they would have had all the support they needed. And something might just have emerged to shake the mighty ruling-class off the backs of the working people.

Young Hen Do you think?

Old Hen I'm sure. And the one man who could see clear through the whole crafty set-up, the one man who said he wouldnae even go to the Palace of Westminster, great John Maclean – oh, hell, did he no' go and die a couple of months later. And that, my girl, was the blackest day of all for the Scottish working-class.

RAMSAY IN POWER

Old Hen Still, onwards and upwards: in a couple of weeks' time they had another election and Labour did even better. The Twentieth-Century

Fox himself, Ramsay MacDonald, did a crafty wee deal with the Liberals, and he was asked to form a Labour government – the hopes were running high in Glasgow, I can tell you. Our own government at last. Jimmy Maxton had a great big victory meeting at Rouken Glen. Me and Charlie had a wee blether wi' him afterwards. He thought parliament was going to change.

Enter JAMES MAXTON *and* CHARLIE. OLD HEN *and* YOUNG HEN *have cleared the set.*

Maxton You see, Charlie, the situation is not exactly cut and dried: the Tories have got more seats than we have, but the Liberals are going to vote against them – so it's certain we *will* be called on to form a government – it's a hell of a tricky.

YOUNG HEN *crosses to them.*

Maxton Hello, my dear – Charlie, is this your . . . ?
Charlie No, no, a good comrade, just a good comrade. We're just good comrades.
Maxton Aye, well, good comrade, have no fear: all your hard work will not be wasted: we won't let you down.
Young Hen I'm sure you won't, Jimmy.
Maxton The big problem is: how to make the wealthy disgorge their wealth. It's gonnae take some doin'.
Charlie Aye, aye.
Maxton We may have to do one or two things the bankers and the Stock Exchange won't like very much – and that means trouble. But we know that wi' folks like you behind us, we cannae go wrong. Keep up the struggle – (*to* YOUNG HEN) – and the hard work, eh, Charlie? (*Goes. Silence.* CHARLIE *starts to go, then stops, embarrassed.*)
Charlie (*To* YOUNG HEN.) Can I see you home?
Young Hen Aye.

They start to walk off. CHARLIE *takes her hand.*

Enter J. RAMSAY MACDONALD *golfing with* GENERAL THOMPSON.

General Thompson Fore! (*Ball flies across stage.* GENERAL THOMPSON *strides off after it.*)
MacDonald My policy paid off – we're in – no thanks to Maxton, the lanky-haired bossy mouth
  And I've come up to think, and play golf, here at Lossiemouth
  I'm choosing my cabinet, and I'm taking advice
  From my friend General Thompson, who's awfully nice.
General Thompson Fore! (*He charges back again after his ball.*)
MacDonald There are those in the party who think I should be democratic
  Consult *them* – that won't work. As Prime Minister one must be – to coin a phrase – more pragmatic:

That means I do what I damn well like, consult who I like,
And blame the workers if anything goes wrong.

General Thompson Fore! (*Crosses yet again after his ball.*)

MacDonald Mind you, I can't understand why he insists on wearing his uniform on the Lossiemouth Golf Course – possibly so he won't get lost in the rough – and talking of getting lost in the rough –

Now, I'm the PM and Foreign Office, too
And I'd be everything else, but there'd be too much to do
I'd have no time for golf or anything.
Good, loyal, right-wingers, in all the key jobs
The problem remains – how to fob off the yobs.

I've had one idea that fits in rather neatly
I'll offer the coal mines to that Bolshevik Wheatley.

WHEATLEY *strides on.*

Wheatley I refuse.

General Thompson Fore!

WHEATLEY *and* J. RAMSAY MACDONALD *crouch as ball flies over.* GENERAL THOMPSON *goes, taking hole with him.* WHEATLEY *also goes.*

MacDonald What one can't win by cunning, one must win by stealth
I'll offer him trouble – Housing and Health.

Wheatley (*Crosses*) I accept. (*He ducks, expecting* GENERAL THOMPSON. *Nothing.*) It's alright, Ramsay.

MacDonald Now I must rush to Aberdeen, avoiding the statue of Wallace –
I've a train to the south, and to Buckingham Palace.

Enter KING GEORGE V *to suitably regal music.*

King George V So we are to call upon a socialist government? Grandmamma would rather jump up on the table and show her knickers.
We suppose we might as well let them play at being Prime Ministers and Home Secretaries, that sort of thing – as far as we can see it won't make any difference to anything serious – our City owns all our money, our industrialists own our industries, our Church owns the minds of our people, and whatever happens, we shall still be king. We have our army, our navy, our air force and our police constables to see to that.

J. RAMSAY MACDONALD *in court dress, bobbing and bowing.*

Ah – J. Ramsay MacDonald – what do you want?

MacDonald Sire, I know the country's not going the way your grandmother meant.
But I really would like to have a wee shot at government.
Just a year or a year and a half, eighteen months, something like that.

King George V Yes, so they tell us. But look here, if you're going to pretend

you're Prime Minister, you must do us the elementary courtesy of cutting
out the silly songs.

MacDonald Sire, there is but one song, sire, I desire, sire, to sing –
    And that, sire, save your reverence – God Save The King.

King George V Yes, we know all that.

MacDonald Do you know the second verse, sir, it's all about the Scots . . . ?

King George V Yes, we are the king – now. You, Mr MacDonald, presided at
    a rally, we think you call it, at Prince Albert's Hall at which our subjects
    sang not only the 'Red Flag', but also – dreadful to relate – the 'Marseil-
    laise'! Today the 'Marseillaise', Mr MacDonald, tomorrow the guillotine.

MacDonald I don't know that one, sire. How does it go?

King George V It's F sharp: with a heavy down-beat – ha-ha.

MacDonald Sire, I *did* protest, I said it was a disgrace.
    But a horrid man from Glasgow told me to shut my face.

King George V Well, don't let it happen again.

MacDonald Only by hard persuasion and clucking like a spinster
    Can I stop the 'Red Flag' being sung in the Palace of Westminster
    But I shall stop their yodelling, from their mouths I'll wean it –
    Or make quite sure that if they do sing, they certainly won't mean it.

King George V Good, we can see you are our man. We, of course, are above
    politics.

MacDonald Yes, we are, sir – –

King George V No, *we* are. Kindly ensure that the rest of your government
    is made up of honest, God-fearing, respectable bum-lickers like yourself,
    or we'll dissolve you.

MacDonald Sire, my earnest – –

King George V (*Shouts*) Get out! We are a busy man!

J. RAMSAY MACDONALD *goes out backwards, bowing.* KING GEORGE V
yawns.

MacDonald My regards to the rest of the family, sire. Sorry to hear about wee
    George's stammer.

King George V We think the neck's safe in the hands of those fools –
    We're off to the Tower to play with our jewels . . .

Goes, humming.

BACKDROP *changes to Glasgow.* MULRINE *living-room is set.*

MEANWHILE, BACK IN GLASGOW

Wheatley (*In spot.*) While politicians are manoeuvering, children are starving,
    mothers weeping, men idle, slums inhabited and wars are being bred.
    While there is one family starving in Scotland, no Clyde Member will
    ca' canny at Westminster. The struggle must not be confined to the
    House of Commons. Labour must mobilize *all* its forces. The millions

who have now voted Labour should be ready to stand or move as Labour calls. All our eggs must not be found in the parliamentary basket.

During WHEATLEY's *speech, scene changes to* HEN's *interior.* CHARLIE *sits in there on his own, looking dejected.* OLD HEN *calls across to* YOUNG HEN, *who has been listening to* WHEATLEY – *and points to* CHARLIE.

Old Hen Psst –!

Young Hen What's up wi' him?

Old Hen Away in and find out; maybe he's waiting for you.

Young Hen Where's my mother?

Old Hen Oot.

Young Hen My faither?

Old Hen Oot.

Young Hen Ma brother?

Old Hen Oot, Oot, Oot – the lot of them. What an opportunity . . .

Young Hen Oh, God aye, you're right – what am I keeping him waiting for?

She goes into the scene.

Hello, Charlie – what're you lookin' so glum for? If you can gie me the answer in less than two hours.

Charlie Oh – this an' that.

Young Hen You feelin' a'right?

Charlie Aye – no' bad.

Young Hen Are you no' even gonnae look at me?

Charlie (*Looks up, smiles.*) Ah, you're no' such a bad sight, hen – and you're a bloody good worker – do you no' resent just doin' the dirty work a' the time?

Young Hen That's what I want to do – I'm no orator – it's worth fighting for, and we fought and won.

Charlie (*Goes back to original gloom.*) Aye.

Young Hen Oh, now what have I said? We've got our *own* government, right? And you and me put them there – right? I thought that's what you wanted.

Charlie (*Angry*) It's a bloody lum-hat government like a' the rest. Listen to this. (*Reads*)

'It is a cabinet of old and ageing men; the average age is nearly sixty. It is a cabinet of dullish men with a large contingent of recruits who have spent most of their lives in the Tory or Liberal parties. It is a cabinet largely of rich men and of men who have inherited comfortable fortunes: of capitalists or landlords or brewers.

'So far as Labour is concerned, many of them have never even worked for their living at all, let alone had experience of poverty. And, as for Socialism, not more than five or six of the whole twenty would call themselves Socialists, and each one of them would give a different definition of that much-abused term . . .' (*Stops reading.*)

Do you want to hear any more? About Lord Haldane or Lord

Parmoor: '... the most dreary and most reactionary of all Tory opponents of social reforms...'?

Young Hen No. I can guess it.

Charlie Or would you like to hear this quote from Carlyle: 'No party has been so sold since Judas concluded his trade'?

Young Hen Still, John Wheatley's in there.

Charlie What the hell can he do, with this lot on his back – he needs pushing, no' pulling does John.

Young Hen Is that what's bothering you?

Charlie No. No' just that. I'm out of work. I've been combed out. Weirs was laying off two hundred – I was number seven. Every red in the shop got thrown out. I get the boot for what? For working to put in a bunch of failed Tories. (*Gets up.*) I'm away to the pub.

Young Hen No, you are not. Sit down or I'll batter you. Right, that's better. Now – what was it you came to see my father about?

Charlie See your father? Oh – well, no – aye ... Er – I didnae come to see your father. Or your mother. Or your brother. I came to see you.

Young Hen Oh aye! What needs doin'?

Charlie Well – nothin' needs doin', so much. (*Pause*) I came to tell you. This is gonnae sound hell of a stupid. No.

Young Hen What?

Charlie Well – I came to tell you that if circumstances had been different, I would have been coming round to say something quite different, but as they are what they are – I'm not.

Young Hen Not what?

Charlie Going to say something quite different.

Young Hen Oh. I see.

Charlie And noo I'm goin'.

Young Hen Wait a minute, I'm still trying to work that out. What *would* you have said if whatever had been whatever?

Charlie No – I'm no' tellin' you that.

Young Hen For Christ's sake – –

Charlie Cheerio. (*Goes.*)

She runs after him and catches him up.

Young Hen Charlie ... were you meanin' – anything personal?

Charlie Och, hell – I luv ye. But I'm broke.

Young Hen Oh, here, that's wonderful ...

Charlie Wonderful?

Young Hen It's really romantic.

Charlie Do you think so? But be a bit practical.

Young Hen Right. I'll be practical. Will you marry me?

Charlie (*Laughs*) You'll have to ask my father ...

Young Hen Come on, let's go down and look at the river. I'm told it's the thing to do – and there's a full moon as well.

They go and look at the river, with ripple-lighting effect used without too
much subtlety over the whole set. MUSIC *in. A romantic song of the period,*
such as 'The Moon Belongs to Everyone', is sung by a smooth SINGER *in a*
tuxedo. An artificial full moon on a stick bobs up and down romantically (?)
behind the Glasgow tenement backdrop. The essence of the song remains:
the trappings – tuxedo, SINGER's *manner, piano style, lighting, moon*
effect, are sent up. On last note of song, LIGHTS *go out.*

The OLD HEN, *who should be playing the piano, mischievously accompany-*
ing her own young romance, gets up as the LIGHTS *come up again.*

Old Hen (*To audience.*) And that was how I got my man, Charlie Sullivan.
(*Enter* YOUNG HEN.)

Young Hen Here, Granny – that was lovely.

Old Hen And did I no' choose the right moment? Not only was he out of
work, he was on the black-list – Weirs had given his name to every
engineering employer in the West of Scotland: troublemaker – no thank
you, get out. And to make matters worse, that wonderful Labour
government we put in did nothing – for Charlie, for me, for naebody.

The only one who got anywhere was Wheatley – he was *determined* to
do something about decent houses for folks to live in, and he got a
start made on that, but even he was no' so sure.

JOHN WHEATLEY *comes on and stands on one side of them.*

Wheatley At the present moment workers' representatives are powerless in
the House of Commons, and I personally do not treat it very seriously,
but regard it as a second- or third-rate debating society. The country is
being driven either to national ruin or bloody revolution.

Old Hen And as for Jimmy Maxton . . .

JAMES MAXTON *comes on the other side, angry.*

Maxton Geordie Buchanan has put up his Home Rule for Scotland Bill.
By Christ I hope it gets through. I want to go to Euston, St Pancras or
Kings Cross, and book a single ticket for Glasgow. I, for one, would be
delighted never to go back to London again. Well – I might go down for
the international, or to hear the Orpheus choir, or something worth-
while – but never for the sake of legislating for the British Empire.

I could ask no greater job in life than to make English-ridden, capitalist-
ridden, landowner-ridden Scotland into the Scottish Socialist Commonwealth – and in doing that, I'd be doing a great service to the people of
England, Wales and the world. (*He and* WHEATLEY *go.*)

Young Hen Here – what happened to that Home Rule Bill?

Old Hen Nothin'. Before they could even castrate it, they were out, the lot of
them – on the burroo, like Charlie. Canny wee Ramsay called another
election, but he wasnae as canny as the Tories. The Tories got back in.
That put the kibosh on it. Enter Winston Churchill and his cronies all

set to smash the workers right back into the ground – six feet under if possible.

They were bitter months, girl, and the unemployment in Glasgow was gettin' worse – Charlie gave up hope of gettin' a job ever again. But still, we were to be married. May nineteen twenty-five. It would have been my Golden Weddin' this year. (*Pauses to think.*) What was I tellin' ye? Aye – we was to be married, an' my mother was all for us stayin' with her – but there was this awfie carry on about sleeping arrangements ...

SLEEPING ARRANGEMENTS

YOUNG HEN *goes into scene as* MOTHER *is talking to* CHARLIE. GEORGE *sits silently.*

Mother Now, Charlie, you've no choice but to stay – and I don't object in the slightest. (GEORGE *stirs.*) Oh, come on now, George, will you stop bloody arguing? Look, before wee Agnes died, you know fine it was Henrietta and Agnes in there, and me and Freddie through there, and you on the floor here. (GEORGE *looks away.*) God grant me patience, you're aye goin' on at me. Alright, so when wee Agnes died me and your father moved in there, Henrietta on the floor here and you got the room to youself. Bloody lucky you were too. I know, you've no need to keep goin' on at me – but surely to Christ you can see that the newlyweds must have the room floor to theirsel's, and you must come in here – it's no gonnae kill you. (GEORGE *sniffs.*) Shut up! I *know* Freddie snores – fit to shake the lums off the roof – I *know* – but if *I* can put up wi' it and she can put up wi' it, so can *you.* (GEORGE *scratches his nose.*) ... George, if you're worried about that, Friday nights you can stay out – God, he's got an answer for everything, so he has.

GEORGE *gets up and goes out.*

(*Shocked*) Where's he off? – Ach, pay no heed to him. He'll come back. You'll both stay wi' us, right? Henrietta's working – she can gie me money for the two of you. ... Now you'll take some potted heid, right, Charlie. Do you know somethin', girl – I've a soft spot for Charlie – you'll need to keep an eye on him. (*She goes off to the kitchen.*)

Charlie I'm sorry, love. I'm – humiliated.

Young Hen You've nothin' to be sorry for, Charlie. I'm sorry for you – no, I'm not sorry. I'm bloody *angry.* And as for that brother of mine – ach, I suppose it was the war.

Charlie I went through the war, too, hen, I had no bloody option.

Young Hen Do you want to tell me about it?

Charlie No. It's just – it wasnae worth it ...

As YOUNG HEN *and* CHARLIE *sit together, uncomfortably, a quiet* SONG *comes in.*

Singer You catch my eye and then you look away –
That secret world you lived in yesterday
Has locked up your heart in some cold prison cell,
Locked me out in the night from your sad private hell –
But a secret despair never dies – won't you tell –
    Have you locked up your heart forever?

You went to war but why you could not say –
Maybe strangers but they were brothers you killed that fine day:
You went out with a gun to shoot men with no name,
Your bayonet tore open bodies with shame
You stifled your cries and your tears and your blame –
    And you locked up your heart forever –

Forget your yesterday
Forget your secret sorrow,
We've love to share today
A new world to build tomorrow:

    And when these wars are of the past
    We'll build a peace that's made to last
    In the world we'll build – tomorrow . . .

The SONG, *or the thoughts that the song has expressed for them both, has drawn them closer together.*

    Enter GEORGE *with suitcase. They watch him as he goes and picks up his bag of tools and dumps them beside the suitcase in the middle of the floor. He pulls his jumping-jack out from under the cupboard and puts it in his pocket.* MOTHER *comes in and watches.*

Mother George, what you doin'?

GEORGE *indicates leaving.*

What do you mean, – goin'? – Where to?

GEORGE, *same gesture.*

Away ta-ta?

Father (*Enters*) What's goin' on here – George, will you no' speak, man?

Pause.

George Aye, I will. The room's gonnae be vacant – if her an him's wantin' to get married, they can sleep in there – it's free – I'm for the aff.

Young Hen George, you don't have to just because . . .

George I've got a room in a boarding house. Five shillins a week includin' washin'. I'm no' stayin' here tae rot – I'm settin' up in business on my own. I've got a wee workshop, and I'll have two carpenters startin' for me Monday morning: do you think I don't mean it?

Mother Look, son, you sit down a wee minute, you'll no' be feeling just too good, eh?

George I've never felt better.

Pause.

Father You need money for that kind of thing, George.

George See that? My bank book. I've been puttin' it away since nineteen nineteen – now I've got what I needed – two hundred pounds – that's capital. I've been workin' for some other man long enough. I've been watchin'. I know how it's done. Now there's gonnae be fellas workin' for me.

Father What are they gonnae do – I mean, what *line*?

George Coffins, doors, wee toys, see . . . (*Shows jumping-jack.*)

Charlie George – can you no' see?

George Aye, I can see – I can see what you and your bloody politics and unions and agitatin's done for us – I can see – I watched and I waited – sure enough – nothin'. You and your schemin's no' gonnae do anything for me till I'm in the ground – so I'm doin' somethin' for mysel' – and I'm gonnae make it – I'm gonnae have a workshop the size of this street, with a yard full of mahogany and ash and walnut and a house, my own house, wi' an inside lavvy, and a front bloody garden, and domestic servants, and a car, with a chauffeur and curtains on the windows and a speakin' tube, and I'm gonnae have a bank account, wi' my money in it – and naebody's gonnae stop me. Because I've planned it.

GEORGE *opens suitcase, takes out overcoat and bowler.*

See: that's mine. That's something, that. (*To* CHARLIE *and* YOUNG HEN.) What you two's dreamin' of is *nothing* – right. I'm gonnae put this on tae walk down the street – and I'm no' coming back.

Mother You're no' coming back?

George I'll send word where you can find me. I'll send you my card.

Father But, son – what are you doin' this for?

George I'm fed up bein' a working-class fool (*Puts on bowler, goes.*)

Mother (*A touch of pride.*) I'm gonnae watch him walk down the street. (*She goes after him.*)

Father For Chris' sake! (*Goes into the other room.*)

Young Hen Does he mean a' that?

Charlie Aye.

Young Hen What are we gonnae do?

Charlie Get married. Sleep in the kitchen. We've no money and no prospects – but we've got somethin', hen – something . . . poor George.

Old Hen An' a' the bairns in the street stopped their play to watch him go.

SINGER *marches into middle of room. Phrase on piano.*

Singer (*Sings*) My maw's a millionaire.

Young Hen/Charlie (*Sing*) Would you believe it?
Singer (*Sings*) Blue eyes, and curly hair,
        Walking down Buchanan Street,
        Wi' her big banana feet,
        Ma maw's a millionaire.

    The whole COMPANY *comes on and sings it again, then sing individually or together:*

Singer   Old Mother Riley at the pawnshop door
        A baby in her arms and a bundle on the floor,
        She asked for ten bob, and she only got four,
        She nearly took the hinges off the old man's door –
All   Our wee school's the best wee school
        The best wee school in Glesa
        The only thing that's wrong wi' it's
        The baldy wee headmaster

        He goes to the pub on a Saturday night
        He goes to the church on Sunday
        He prays to the Lord to gie him strength
        Tae belt the weans on Monday.
Singer   The Big Ship was leaving Bombay –
          today –
        Bound for the Isle of Man
          so they say –
        Along came Henrietta with tears in her eyes,
        Along came Charlie with two big black eyes,
        Saying:
Charlie Darling oh Darling be mine, be mine,
        I'll send you a sweet Valentine:
Singer   He turned round to kiss her,
        She ducked and he missed her –
All   The Big Ship was leaving Bombay – Today.
George If you see a big fat wumman
        Staunin' on the corner bummin'
        (*Stamp*) That's ma mammy.
        If you see a wee thin fella
        Like a rolled-up umbrella
        (*Stamp*) That's ma daddy.
Young Hen When oor da' gets another job
        Each week he'll earn fifty bob
        We'll a' be like folk in Bearsden
        Wi' carpet flairs an' lavvies ben
        In and oot the Parish
        In and oot the Parish

In and oot the Parish
God bless the Unemployed.
Like Mary Rae who jeers us all
We'll wear a coat an' no' a shawl
The plates o' peas we'll leave alone
For we'll hae links an' tattie scones

In and oot the Parish, etc.

Oor maw will hae a stuck-up nose
For we will stay in a wally close
We'll be sae rich an' no' the same
We'll even ken the factor's name.

In and oot the Parish, etc.

Father There is a happy land down Duke Street Jail
Where a' the prisoners stand, tied to a nail
Ham and eggs they never see
Dirty water for their tea
That's the place for you and me
God Save the Queen.

Old Hen Oh ye cannae shove yer grannie off a bus
All Quite right, too
Old Hen No ye cannae shove yer grannie off a bus
Oh ye cannae shove yer grannie
Young Hen For she's yer mammy's mammy
Old Hen No ye cannae shove yer grannie off a bus.

    ALL *sing this again as one of the* COMPANY *says that it's interval time, and there's a bar, so I will if you will, so will I* . . .

All Singing I will if you will so will I
Singing I will if you will so will I
Singing I will if you will
I will if you will,
I will if you will, so will I.

                                 INTERVAL

ACT II

As LIGHTS *go down,* CHARLIE *and* FATHER *come on to room set and pace anxiously up and down.*

OLD HEN *comes on shouting for* HENRIETTA, *who is amongst the audience.*

Old Hen Have you seen that girl? She's never here when I want her. Henrietta, where the hell are you? Are you down there selling shares in Scotland's oil?

Young Hen Gie's a break.

Old Hen I'm wantin' you.

Young Hen I'm busy.

Old Hen It's the young men you're after, is it? Put that man down, he's old enough to be your grandfather.

Young Hen I'm just sortin' out these Liberals (*in the circle/at the bar/over here, etc.*).

Old Hen Liberals? In here? God, if there's one thing worse than a Tory it's a Liberal – where are they – I'll sort them out mysel'.

Young Hen No, Gran. I've given them a good speakin'-to, they'll no' cause any bother. (*Comes up on to stage.*)

Old Hen Right – now I've a wee bit more to tell you before I'm done. See these two here?

Young Hen What's up wi' them?

Old Hen Nineteen twenty-six! And the house of Mulrine is in a state of high nervous tension ...!
   Was it because of the unemployment?

Charlie/Father (*Together*) No.

Old Hen Was it because there was a Tory government intent on smashing the workers?

Charlie/Father (*Together*) No.

Old Hen Was it because capitalism was entering an almighty crisis, a deep depression, a black despair?

Charlie/Father (*Together*) No.

Young Hen What was it then?

Old Hen Sssh!

A baby's cry, from off. MUSIC *in,* CHARLIE *jumps up in the air with delight, and* FATHER *shakes his hand.* CHARLIE *comes down to sing: 'You Can Come and See the Baby', a Will Fyfe number – or another suitable old song to celebrate the birth of a baby – father's version. The* FAMILY *join in the last chorus. At the end,* CHARLIE *is led in by* MOTHER, *to see the baby.*

Old Hen Aye. Only thing was – it was a girl. Joan – your mother.

Young Hen Oh, God – here, my mother was born in that house? Wi' her father out of work? You're kiddin' me on . . .

Old Hen Do you think I'm likely to forget?

Young Hen And she's the one that's tellin' me how I ought to meet some nice young men, so why don't I join the Young Conservatives?

Old Hen Aye, well, she's come up in the world, eh – got herself a high-rise flat in Garngad – –

Young Hen Oh no, we don't call it that any more – it's known as Royston Hill now we've moved in . . . the man up the stair's daein' eight years for armed robbery and the fella down the stair's daein' life for sawin' heads off wi' a hacksaw – but to hear my mother you'd think it was some sort of upper-class monastery.

Old Hen She's been a pain in the backside ever since she went scrubbin' floors in Newton Mearns . . .

Young Hen Did you know Mrs Tomlinson drove her through to Edinburgh, and the pair of them stood wavin' Union Jacks at Margaret Thatcher?

Old Hen God – what a stimulatin' experience – ach, the working-class has aye had problems like Joan: the problem is most of them end up on the General Council of the TUC. And the year she was born was the year that lot came out in their true colours . . . nineteen twenty-six. I was a shop steward at the time, and when I got back to the sweatshop after your mother was born, I could see the way things were going: the system was in trouble, trade was no' boomin', even the coal owners were losin' money – so *we* were under attack. The only thing between them and us was the unions. Somebody had to stand up and say NO. As usual it was the miners – right out in front, ready to take a batterin'.

THE IMPLACABLE FOE

(*Continues.*) But they were nae just havin' a go at the miners. Big Chief Baldwin spilt the beans, when some of the miners went to see him . . .

BALDWIN *and* MINER *come on, try to pass each other, do, then recognise each other.*

Baldwin Ah, you're a coal-miner.

Miner Ah, you're a Prime Minister.

Baldwin Yes. Now then, industry is confronted with a difficult situation. You chaps will just have to jolly well make your contribution.

Miner Do you mean get oor wages cut?

Baldwin Yes, I do. All the workers in this country have got to face a reduction in wages.

Miner A reduction in wages? What do you mean?

Baldwin I mean – I shall say it again, and every Prime Minister including your own Bolshevik Harold Wilson will say it after me.

Miner You can say that again.

Baldwin I shall say it again and every Prime Minister including your own Bolshevik Harold Wilson will say it after me. I mean all the workers in this country have got to take reductions in wages to help put British industry on its feet.

Miner Is that a fact? Well, I say to you and every British miner will say it after me – get knotted!

Baldwin You'd better not say that again.

Miner Get knotted. Twice.

They go off.

Old Hen Aye, capitalism was buggered; just like it is now. And the only way they could make it work was to take money out of the pockets of the workers. Just like it is now. The only consolation then was that it was a Tory government.

Young Hen Just like it is now.

Old Hen So you can tell a Tory when you see one?

Young Hen Aye – –

Old Hen Except when it's in a kilt – –

Young Hen Will you get on with the story, and stop provokin' me? She's a bigot, so she is.

Old Hen Every trade unionist in the country rallied to defend the miners, right? Not a minute on the day, not a penny off the pay – right? Or the whole country's coming out – right? Ya bas. The Tories beat a crafty retreat: OK – the subsidy will go on to the first of May nineteen twenty-six. They were giving themselves time to prepare for a fight. And they intended to win, so by the first of May 1926 they were ready. But were we?

Enter J. RAMSAY MACDONALD.

MacDonald As far as we can see we shall go on. I don't like General Strikes. I haven't changed my opinion. I have said so in the House of Commons. I don't like it; honestly: I don't like it; but, honestly, what can be done?

By the way, I'm the leader of the Labour Party. Honestly.

Mrs Beatrice Webb Poor Ramsay! Dear Diary – 'We personally are against the use of the General Strike in order to force the government to submit to the men's demands. If it were to succeed it would mean a militant minority were starving the majority into submission – and that would be the end of democracy.'

By the way, my husband agrees with me – and he's chairman of the Labour Party. Come on, Ramsay – (*produces handkerchief*) – big blow– (*He blows. They go.*)

Old Hen The diddy men . . . Aye, but it wasnae just the politicians. The miners' leaders stood firm as a rock, but they had to put the matter in the hands of the General Council of the British TUC.

Enter, to MUSIC, *some of the General Council of the TUC, 1926.*

TUC (*Sing*) We're the British TUC, TUC, TUC
        We're the British TUC, let's do a deal –
        We don't want a revolution
        To change the constitution
        That's not our cuppa tea you see

        – Let's do a deal –

        The Tories aren't waiting
        While we're cogitating
        Volunteers they are massing
        While we sit here gassing
        They've organisations
        To run railway stations
        They've student tram-drivers
        With monocles and fivers
        They've black-leg coal miners
        Protest and they'll fine us –

        Our members have pleaded
        That we do what's needed

        So we formed a Committee
        But Oh what a pity

        We're the British TUC
        We've done sod all.

Walter Citrine Comrades and friends – I don't like saying that, but I've got to – my name is Walter Citrine. I'm not a Lord yet, but I bloody soon will be – meantime I'm the General Secretary of this outfit. The union members are trying to tell us what to do – they want a General Strike. But *I* say what goes, that's what I'm paid for. We'll negotiate a settlement – on behalf of the miners – won't we, lads?

Others Aye, Walter, aye, Walter, aye aye aye.

Citrine Not that I'm not democratic: oh no – TUC does not stand for Trampled Under Citrine, as some wit remarked. God rest his soul. No – it means Tolerance – under Citrine. So they can all shut their cake-holes, I don't fancy General Strikes, too much paper work. Let's go and do a deal with Baldwin while the miners aren't looking. I like going to Number Ten Downing Street, you get your picture in the paper – come on, lads...

Baldwin (*In pyjamas and top hat.*) Negotiations are broken off. And I've gone to bed. Go away. (*Produces teddy-bear.*) Come on, Teddy. (*Goes.*)

Citrine Oh dear – now we're for it. ....

All (*Sing*) They've soldiers, and sailors
        Policemen and gaolers

They'll surely defeat us –
Then Churchill will eat us . . .
    AArgh! – for breakfast, on toast.
They'll come for you and me, you see –
    Let's do a deal.

They go off in terror.

Old Hen That Executive grovelled, it cringed, it begged Baldwin to think of a way to stop them calling a General Strike. That was when Baldwin and Churchill and Lord Birkenhead and the other generalissimos of the ruling class knew they were on a winner. Their side was organised, ours was unprepared, feart, and weak at the top. Go ahead – says Baldwin – call your strike – and we'll smash you.

Enter CHARLIE *to house, with blood pouring from his head.*

Mother (*Off*) Is that you, Freddie? (*Comes on.*) Charlie!! What in the name of . . . Come here till I see. (FATHER *comes in.*) Freddie, will you get a cloth or somethin'?

Charlie Ach, I'm alright . . .

Father What happened to you?

Charlie Nothin' – we heard there was blackleg tram-drivers in Dalmarnock tram depot – about four or five hundred miners from Newton and Cambuslang came in tae help us picket the place, that's all . . .

Mother So who walloped you?

Charlie There was more bloody polis than I've ever seen in the whole of my life. They came down on us like a pack of wolves – look at that . . . (*Shows jacket ripped right up the back.*)

Father Never mind that – what about that? (*His head*)

Charlie I'm no' feelin' just so steady on my pins . . .

Mother Oh Christ, where's the lassie?

Charlie She's away to Carlton Place, to give the word to the Trades Council – on a bicycle.

Mother On a bicycle – but she cannae ride one –

Charlie She's just found out.

Mother Here, I'll get you somethin' to wash yoursel'. (*Goes.*)

Charlie D'you hear about they students in Edinburgh? Tried to drive a train – Christ knows how but they smashed it up in a tunnel – three people got killed.

Father Aye – it's a terrible thing.

MOTHER *comes back with rag.*

Mother Here, I'm that worried about that lassie.

Charlie Och, she'll be alright – oh Christ! That bike.

Mother What?

Charlie Well, it's just – I told her how tae go it, but I didnae tell her how to stop . . .

Old Hen (*Laughing*) But I found out all by myself – when I got tae Jamaica Bridge there was this wee student in plus-fours tryin' to direct the traffic – he'd volunteered so the real polis could go and crack a few skulls – I thought to mysel' right, you wee bastard – and I drove straight at him, yellin' help, help, I cannae stop, I cannae stop! and the gallant wee manny haulds out his hand, and I grabs it – well … (*sings*) He flew through the air with the greatest of ease – and I fell off; another casualty in the class war.

And all over England and Wales and Scotland, the strike got bigger and better organised, and stronger – you see, we were sure we were goin' to win. We had tae – we knew what wis waitin' for us if we lost …

LIGHTS *change*. TWO MEMBERS *of* COMPANY *come on to read, as themselves, from newspapers, etc., of the time.* (*These readings can vary to suit locality of performance.*)

1st Reader The main unions called out in support of the miners were the railwaymen, the transport workers, the builders, the iron and steel workers. After one week of the strike, the printers, engineers and shipyard workers came out. In all cases, the strikes were almost one hundred per cent solid.

2nd Reader *British Gazette,* the official organ of the government during the strike. 'All ranks of the Armed Forces of the Crown are hereby notified that any action which they may find it necessary to take in an honest endeavour to aid the Civil Power will receive both now and afterwards the full support of His Majesty's Government.'

1st Reader Cardinal Bourne: 'There is no moral justification for a General Strike. It is therefore a sin against the obedience which we owe to God. All are bound to uphold and assist the Government which is the lawfully constituted authority of the country and represents, therefore, the authority of God himself.'

2nd Reader Lord Reith, General Manager of the BBC, to Mr Baldwin: 'Assuming that the BBC is for the people, and that the government is for the people, it follows that the BBC must be for the government.'

1st Reader American observer at London docks: 'I saw enough artillery to kill every living thing in every street in the neighbourhood.'

2nd Reader Sir John Simon, former Liberal Home Secretary: 'Every trade union leader is liable in damages to the uttermost farthing of his personal possessions.'

1st Reader The Hon. Mrs Beaumont undertook stable duties at Paddington Station.

2nd Reader Unemployed car salesman: 'I'd always been mad on model railways, and of course, my dream was to drive a train. I was really in my element.'

1st Reader A train which left Manchester on Tuesday at nine-thirty a.m. is reported to have arrived in London at ten-fifteen a.m. Friday.

2nd Reader Undergraduate: 'We set out from Oxford early in the evening in a vintage Bentley and drove at great speed through the lovely English countryside. At Doncaster our driver stood us dinner and a bottle of champagne. From Doncaster onwards, groups of strikers tried to interrupt our progress by occasionally throwing stones and trying to puncture our tyres. However, our driver remained unperturbed and merely accelerated when he saw a hostile crowd – at times we reached eighty miles an hour. On the following day I started work on Glasgow docks.'

The THREE ACTORS *in the scene have been listening. They now break in.*

3rd Reader (Charlie) Peter Kerrigan, Glasgow Trades Council, Strike Coordinating Committee: (And you'll no' find this in the *British Gazette*.) 'The majority of strike-breakers in Glasgow were recruited from the students. They tried to move lorries from the docks and man trams, mainly in the centre. But they couldn't move half a mile without being smashed up and the lorries from the docks had to have a military escort. It was a long time before what the students did was forgotten.'

4th Reader (Father) R. E. Scoular, STUC: 'In and out of the city not a vehicle could move without our sanction. We would have commercial travellers ringing us up highly indignant at being waylaid by gangs of miners. I had an anxious phone-call from one of the pickets – 'What shall we do, the field's full?' 'What field?' 'We're stopping the cars on the road and turning them into a field.' 'Well, find another field.'

3rd Reader (Charlie) Glasgow: eleventh of May nineteen twenty-six. One hundred persons were sentenced to three months' imprisonment, twenty-five for longer. Fourteen were from Maryhill, accused of taking part in a disturbance: a procession of young men through the streets, headed by a man playing a melodeon, shouting 'To Hell with the Government' – and other remarks.

4th Reader (Father) Will Blyton, Durham miner: 'The Dean of Durham made a speech saying that the miners were never satisfied. We marched in with banners saying "To Hell With Bishops, We Want a Living Wage". The women were so infuriated they pushed him in the river. That night he preached a sermon on the text: Father, forgive them for they know not what they do.'

5th Reader (Young Hen) Megan Morgan, South Wales: 'It was beautiful weather that summer, what we call strike weather. It never seemed to rain. Some nights there would be dancing in the streets half the night. The jazz bands would walk from the Rhondda half-starved as they were. We dammed up the river, made a pool and there was bathing by moonlight. Everything was organised: the soup-kitchen, even the boat-repairing was done co-operatively.

3rd Reader (Charlie) Dutch, German and Czech miners all solid in support of the British miners. The Canadian, American, French, German, All-India and Russian TUCs sent donations. All accepted – except the Russian, which was sent back.

The three in the scene return to their set.

1st Reader Twelfth of May: Deeside – no sign of weakening.
2nd Reader Twelfth of May: Kilmarnock – not the slightest sign of weakening.
1st Reader Twelfth of May: Denny and Dunipace – no weakening.
2nd Reader Twelfth of May: Bo'ness – no weakening.
1st Reader Twelfth of May: Bermondsey, London – no sign of weakening whatever.
2nd Reader Twelfth of May: Birkenhead – no weakening, stoppage extending.
1st Reader Twelfth of May: Wolverhampton – no weakening.
2nd Reader Twelfth of May: Wakefield – no sign of weakening.
1st Reader Twelfth of May: Glasgow . . .

Back into house. ALL *there, as before.* YOUNG HEN *runs in with a newspaper.*

Young Hen Here, look at that.
Charlie What are you doin' readin' that scab's daily for?
Young Hen Read it . . .
Charlie What does it say?
Young Hen It says the strike's called off. The General Council of the TUC has given in – unconditional surrender.
Charlie Ach away – –
Young Hen It's been announced on the wireless, Charlie – it's *true* – and the bosses are ecstatic – listen . . .
    'Not since Armistice Day has the city heard any news which has given greater satisfaction.' Then inside – 'No union member formerly employed on the *Glasgow Herald* need apply for re-instatement.'
Charlie So they've begun already . . .
Father For what have they stopped it?
Charlie (*Forcefully, angrily.*) I don't know.
Mother Still an' all, thank God it's all over.
Charlie You'll no' be thanking God in a month or two, Nora, we're all gonnae suffer – we've fought and we've lost – now we're gonnae pay the price. As if we're not paying enough already – the whole working class is gonnae suffer for this for years to come.

They go off, leaving OLD HEN. YOUNG HEN *joins her, and listens, in a quiet, intimate grouping that draws them together.*

BONE SOUP

Old Hen Aye, and so we did. Soon Charlie wasnae the only one on the parish – there was thousands and thousands queueing for their dole-money – if they were lucky enough to get any. We got another Labour government alright – aye, Ramsay MacDonald rode again – we put him in to increase the benefit – do you know what he did? He cut it. When he came in, one man in ten was unemployed – in two years, one man in five. Do you know what we had to dae? Ah've seen my ain mother traipse on her two feet frae Bridgeton to Skinners in Sauchiehall Street, wi' a pillow-slip tae fill wi' broken loaves that naebody wanted – and, if she was lucky, squashed meringues. The next day she'd be up to the Bermaline for two pennorth of broken biscuits. First Charlie lost his job, then my father, then my mother – I was still going on fine, nineteen shillings a week frae the sweatshop, stitching up ball-gowns and pin-stripe suits. Made me sick to think of people dressin' up like that wi' other people starvin' near to death in the same city – still, it was keepin' me in work: till then what happened? Just what I needed maist in the world – twins.

Young Hen You mean my Uncle Freddie in Vancouver?

Old Hen Aye, and your Uncle Charlie that was washed away in the floods in Darwin, Australia. Here, did he no' send you a boomerang?

Young Hen Aye. It didnae work.

Old Hen I fed them till they were five months; I was like a rake. I heard you got one and sixpence a week extra frae the parish if you were feeding a wain . . . the bastard asked me if I could prove it – I felt like whippin' one out and gie'n him a squirt in the eye. Still, we got by. Mince and tatties on a Thursday and there was aye bone-soup – if you could get a bone that is. It was hard to get a bone . . . see Jessie Nolan, her they've stuck in the Eventide Home – well she had this great big knee-bone: Here, says I – what kind of a beast did you get that off of, an elephant out of the zoo? Don't let on, says she. Here, I says, gie's a lend of it after you've finished with it. Three pots of soup came out of that bone – it went from her pot tae mine, and then tae May Armstrong up the stair – and that's God's truth.

Ach, the thirties was nae time to be trying to get by, in Glasgow or anywhere else – they *had* to start another war, to get the men some work. And our great parliamentary heroes? What did they do? Most of the Great Reds of the Clyde slid into the Labour Party, in the hope of turnin' into Prime Ministers. Not Jimmy Maxton, no – he became a sad, solitary voice, crying in the wilderness. Nor Wheatley. He died. Still a Pape, but still fightin'. And the TUC? Spineless. And then, to cap it all, doesnae Charlie decide he's going off to Spain to do battle with the Fascists? Oh aye – it was the right courageous thing to dae. But was there no' enough to fight here? I telt him – if anyone's gonnae get shot, it'll be you – but no – he knew. Well, I was proved right by a Fascist bullet, wallop, right between the eyes – he was aye pig-headed. Leaving me wi' three wains to bring up – if I could have got a haud of him, I'd have kicked his heed in.

Poor Charlie; we need a few more like him today.

OLD HEN *is by now very upset about Charlie.* YOUNG HEN *gently leads her off. Song, to tune 'Jamies Foyers', the first verse of Ewan MacColl's song:*

Singer   He's gone frae the shipyard that stands on the Clyde
             His hammer is silent, his tools laid aside;
             To the wide Ebro River, young Foyers has gone
             To fecht by the side of the people of Spain.

She turns and watches GEORGE *come on, then goes.*

LET'S GO WITH LABOUR

GEORGE *comes into kitchen, looks around, sniffs, mutters. He looks prosperous and bigger.*

George Nineteen fifty-one. Well, this is one part of Britain that's not havin' a festival. Pig-sty. To think that in nineteen fifty-one they old folks is still living like pigs. (*To audience.*) I was brought up in this house. Thank Christ we're livin' in a democracy where a fella like me can get out of slums like this. Take me for example. Brother Charlie got a bullet in Spain. I've got a villa. And I come frae *this*. That's democracy.

The last time you clapped your eyes on me, I was settin' up in wood – wee toys, coffins, doors. Well you can keep your wee toys and coffins – they're for kids and corpses, neither of which is particularly big spenders. Doors, that's what held the key. Doors go intae buildings, right – so do door-frames, window-frames, roof-beams, floorboards, flights of stairs and fitted cupboards – the buildin' industry: the only industry apart frae armaments that was booming in the nineteen thirties. I began to get wee contracts for Corporation housing schemes; Knightswood, Carntyne – then I met a bent quantity surveyor on holiday in Largs. We began to see eye to eye, and my contracts expanded. Now I'm married to his daughter, Priscilla – I think that's her name – and I'm daein' very well thank you. Durin' the war I diversified; into Nissen huts, air-raid shelters and officers' messes: important war-work. And thanks to your wee boy, Adolf Hitler, I made a packet. Pre-fabs. Rebuildin'.

After the war, we got ourselves this Labour government – wi' big plans. I began to see the positive aspects of John Wheatley's housing schemes – if you know what I mean? The Glasgow Corporation seemed set on spending millions of pounds on buildings. I felt, at this point, I needed some political representation myself – so I joined the Labour Party – well, I'm a working-class boy – and got myself elected a councillor. And, now, due to my specialist know-how, I'm on the Building Committee – you might think – in fact you probably certainly do think – I'd have a conflict of interests there – me bein' a contractor to the Corporation an' that, but believe me, there was no conflict – my interests went hand in hand together. But the Moving Finger writes, and having wrote moves

on. Now we're into the golden days: Easterhouse, Castlemilk, Drum-
chapel, Pollock – I'm employin' six hundred men, I cannae go wrong.
And now we've started makin' plans for the big one. Enough of mucking
around in the suburbs – the whole of the city awaits.

The future lies glowing ahead like a Christmas puddin'. First, a few
bob on the side renovatin' the old tenements – that's Phase One. Phase
Two, you sell them to Glasgow Corporation. Phase Three, Glasgow
Corporation pays you to knock them all down, and Phase Four, and
this is where the real profits, or should I say social benefits, come in – you
pay me to rebuild the whole shooting-match. Share this vision with me
now – mile upon mile of motorway threadin' its way through the elegant,
tree-dotted landscapes of Anderston, Partick and Govan, where a con-
tented population dwells in tall, slender towers, shopping effortlessly in
spacious shopping centres with purpose-built access roads – and all this
due, false modesty be damned, to yours truly, Baillie George Mulrine
placing contracts with Mulrine (Motorways) Ltd; Mulrivert (Vertical
Dwelling Units) Ltd; Mulriscape (Environmental Sculptors) Ltd; Mul-
ristorey Car Parks; and Mulresco (Easyspend Trading Arcades). So
come on, boys: Let's Go With Labour.

Enter MOTHER *and* FATHER, *very old and frail.*

Mother Who's that?
Father Eh?
Mother There's a man . . .
George Do you not recognise me? Aye, well, I suppose I must have changed.
Mother George! It's my own George – oh, here, son, you're lookin' awful
well. (*Admires him.*)
Father What have you come for?
George What have I come for? – to see *you* of course.
Father Oh, aye . . .
Mother Oh, that's lovely, I knew you'd come back.
George And to bring you some news – we're gonnae knock your house
down – –
Father You're gonnae what?
George But first, we're gonnae do it up. Would you like that?
Mother Oh, aye, I suppose we would.
George Right, sign here, you can pay in instalments. (*Shouts*) Right, lads –
in here – shift yourselves.

Enter BUILDERS, *who transform the set under* GEORGE's *supervision –
modern sink,* TV *set, new chairs, dining recess, new purple nylon curtains,
new wallpaper, etc.* MOTHER *and* FATHER *watch, amazed, appalled. At the
end they all look at it. Finally, they turn* FATHER's *head to the* TV.

George Right, lads, every house in the close and every close in the street,
then you can get your dinner. (*They go.*)

Mother Here, George, don't you get upset – that's very nice.

George It's for you, Mother – it's what Jimmy Maxton, John Wheatley, John Maclean – my forebears in the Labour movement was dreaming of for the working classes. Did you sign that paper?

Mother Aye.

George Right, well – I must go now – Mulrinauld (New Towns) Ltd is startin' up in a year or two – I'm away to look at a few fields on the road to Stirling – so I'll be seein' you – and don't forget to pay your rates. (*Goes.*)

Mother It's very nice, very nice.

Old Hen (*To* YOUNG HEN) And that is how what is now known as socialism finally came to the Clyde.

ENTER SCOTLAND'S OIL

Old Hen There you are, my girl, that's my story – I saw Scotland on the move, hen – it began with hundreds of thousands of people on the streets of Glasgow singing the 'Red Flag', demanding socialism. It ended wi' this shemozzle we've got now – a string of Labour governments doing the Tories' job for them, and the TUC doing the bosses' job for them: one and a quarter million people out of work. And Glasgow? . . . well . . . that's my story.

Young Hen Here, Gran, that's a terrible story, so it is – but do you no' think you've left out a few bits?

Old Hen The bits I've left out would keep you here a' night – how that Labour government of Attlee's sold its soul for a few million dollars of Marshall Aid – and if I got on tae Harold Wilson and Reginald Prentice: in the name of – –

Young Hen No, no, no, I was meaning the good bits – I mean folks *do* have better houses and mair food in their belly, and better dole money and better wages now than they used to . . .

Old Hen Oh aye, after the war we got quite a lot started. There's a wee bit to show for a' these years, batterin' away. I should bloody hope so. But do you remember Jimmy Maxton? John Wheatley? Willie Gallacher? What they stood for? Do you remember John Maclean – what he died for? No' a few bob here and a high-rise flat there, hen – no: never that – surely we're no' gonnae be satisfied with that – it's *life* we're talking about: how everybody can make the most of the short short time they've got to live. No' just a few people – everybody. That's what socialism's about.

Young Hen That's what we all want, Gran – –

Old Hen Aye, but do we all *fight* for it? Do we know *how* to fight for it? Do we have the weapons – organisation and discipline? Or the ammunition – words – and action? Do we *think*? Do we learn? Do we dae anything at all for what we want? Thank Christ *some* do – but where's the others?

Young Hen You did your bit, eh, Gran?

Old Hen Ach, I wasnae anything special, there wis thousands like me – I did what I could, and it wasnae much. It wasnae enough, and I'm still waving a solitary red flag on the number nine bus! And I'm still handin' out bloody pamphlets – here – there's gonnae be a big rally to get that Shrewsbury picket out of gaol – and we *will*, too.

Young Hen Are you no' gettin' just a wee bit cynical?

Old Hen No I am not. I'm busy and I'm waitin'. For you lot to *see*. And to dae something better – –

Young Hen Us? Christ, you've near put me off altogether . . .

Old Hen Are you talkin' about givin' up? Never. You haven't even started yet. Now – what I'm wantin' to know from you is – just what do you propose to do that's any different?

Young Hen Me?

Old Hen Aye, *you* – and that so-called political party of yours – the Bay City Rollers of Westminster – –

Young Hen Don't you say one word against the Bay City Rollers – they may be bourgeois pigs, but they're loved.

Lighting change. Screams (on tape) from speakers. A POP-GROUP *rush on with cut-out guitars, drums, mike. Nod to tape-operator.* MUSIC *blasts out. They mime to it, out of sync.*

Group You see our smiles in the papers
The fans all scream and swoon
You see us holdin' a cardboard guitar
Somebody else plays the tune.

Drum break. Three SNP POLITICIANS *come on and try to join in the trendy merry-making.*

It's a revelation
The way we wear our jeans –
SNP Politicians It's a revolution
Since we came on the scene –
All And we're laughin' all the way to the bank
For though we know we're just ornamental
Nothing more than a monumental – prank –
To be frank . . .
We're the craze,
We're the craze,
Nowadays,
We're the craze.

Repeat last four lines to fade. GROUP *go, leaving three* POLITICIANS *waving them off. The three SNP politicians are* CHARLOTTE SQUARE, *an Edinburgh lady enthusiast,* HAMISH BANFF, *from the North-east, and* WILLIAM MCCASHIN, *an Edinburgh lawyer.*

MRS CHARLOTTE SQUARE *steps forward as* GROUP *goes, and screams fade.*

Mrs Charlotte Square Wonderful, wonderful. Our boys. So full of vitality, and talent. Now: hello. My name is Mrs Charlotte Square. And I believe that we in the SNP have all of Scotland's ills firmly rooted in our minds. And we are all set to get shot of them altogether.

Now. Tonight we have two – or should I say 'twa' – speakers, who will, I am sure, make our hearts beat just that little bit faster. So without more ado, I am proud to introduce to you one of our own dear MPs – Mr Hamish Banff.

She goes and sits, as HAMISH BANFF *steps forward, producing typewritten sheet from his pocket, from which he constantly breaks off to give his personal philosophy.*

Hamish Banff Thank you, thank you – er – thank you, Madam Chairman. (*Reads*) 'Greetings, fellow Scots, patriots and sons of Caledonia.' By the way, my name is Hamish Banff, and I'm a couthie wee Nat. Now I have a wee speech here from Party Headquarters I'd like to read to you – 'Dear Hamish – please stick to the speech' – No, no, that's personal – here it is now – 'Scotland's own dear soil is very precious to me –' oh aye, he's nae telling me naething – I farm eight hundred acres of the best of it – it's no' been a bad year. The bullocks was a bit slow at the beginning but by God they came on at the hinner end. This may have had something to do with the tremendous high price of the barley we kept back from last year's crop. Now I'm not saying we caused prices to fluctuate, but we covered our costs. But keep on complaining, lads. It's the only way to make a spare bob. Now: 'Do not be misled by the propaganda of the London parties – Labour, Liberal or Conservative' – I was a Conservative myself as a matter of fact, stood for parliament for them a few years back; but I soon realised the error of my ways – I didnae get in. Ach, the Tories is done in Scotland. Not patriotic enough. Bloody namby-pamby stuff wi' no grit – nothing but haute couture and perfume: I mean Margaret's alright on the floor of the House or in a lobby but could she handle your bullocks – Mind you, she certainly intends to keep a firm grip on the workers – but: let her come to grips with the English workers and leave the Scottish working man to us – Where was I? Oh aye, propaganda – 'do not be mislead by the propaganda of the London parties, we in Scotland are on the road to untold riches' – well, some of us have got untold riches right now, and as long as they remain untold, there'll be no more questions asked. You see – we need the business fraternity as our friends, make no mistake about that – and that is why we've gone to the trouble to set up our Economics Advisory Committee – with your boys from the merchant banks and the investment trusts and the Stock Exchange – to tell us exactly how to run Scotland – and make a profit: no skimping – these are the best men – when it comes to making a bob or two – and after independence that's what we'll all be in it for – er, in for. 'We are going to give Scottish businessmen a fair crack of the whip.' Now I realise that's a dangerous image that, but we're no' sayin' who's back we're cracking it on. I'll say this, though, you won't see the blood for the colour of the shirt.

Aye, and we'll have the labourers back in the bothies singing bothy ballads and snapping up their bowl of brose, that's what made Scotland great, not wasting their time chasing better wages like they do in England. All these realities will become a dream when our own dear Scotia becomes a nation once again. Thank you. (*Sits*)

MRS CHARLOTTE SQUARE *gets up, applauding.*

Mrs Charlotte Square Thank you, Hamish. What a rugged wee Scot you are. Now I'm going to hand you over to a *real thinker*. Scotland's answer to Sir Alec Douglas Home – and all the other great political philosophers of the twentieth century.

I think you're going to appreciate what this man has to offer – I know I do – here he is – a man who needs no introduction . . .

Sits, as WILLIAM MCCASHIN *rises to speak.*

McCashin Fellow Scots, others. William McCashin speaking. As things looked quite promising for this great movement of ours, I thought I'd better join it. I'm a thinker, and an Edinburgh lawyer. So I'm a pretty quick thinker.

Now many witless people, some having the misfortune to be non-Scottish, have accused us of not having any policies. That's not true. We have. I remember them well. In fact I have them written on the back of this piece of paper. I will put them to you in the form of questions and answers. In that order, question, then answer. Thus you might well ask: What is your policy on housing? You might well ask that. Well, our policy is: After independence there will be housing in Scotland. But it will be Scottish housing – that just about covers that one.

Now, we don't need, as a party, to go into details. It's obvious that, after independence, the details will be worked out.

What – next question – what is your policy on the economy? Answer: After independence, the Scottish economy will boom – But that's not all – no, wait for it – thanks to our oil. I mean – would you rather be Rich and Scottish, or Poor and English? Any fool could answer that one. Several fools have.

I mean, now we've got our oil – well, now the multi-national oil companies have got our oil – there must be a bob or two in it for you and me. Preferably a bob for you and two for me. (*Laughs*) No, no. Surely the Americans will slip us the odd quid here and there. Now – nationalisation. I say no – the Americans wouldn't like it. So forget about nationalisation. After independence – don't offend the Americans, and support Scottish bosses. That's not a policy, by the way, that's just stating the obvious. Next question: Is the SNP a left-wing or a right-wing party? The simple answer to that is yes. And no. We simply think up the policies that are right for Scotland – and that, of course, has nothing to do with politics. Now there are a lot of people, including rank-and-file members of the SNP – even one or two optimistic vice-chairmen, going round saying After independence, Scotland will be socialist. Now, I don't want to scare you people, but socialism means secret police, massacre of women and children, rape, arson, looting, thuggery, monumental architecture, anarchy, chaos, civil war, American intervention possibly with H-bombs, the death of all we hold near and dear – and workers getting more wages. Now this last one's the real problem. So we've thought of a policy to deal with that. After independence, Scotland will definitely not be a socialist country. Though of course there is still a high level of democratic discussion – in the East Kilbride Branch.

No, we will put an end to dividing Scotsman from fellow Scotsman. After all, Hugh Fraser is just the same, under the kilt, as any common old working chap. And Glasgow belongs to both of them. What do they both want? Money. Well, our New Politics rises above class-wars and divisiveness, and all that out-dated political jargon – and says we must all get together to make money for Hugh Fraser.

That is my glimpse into the future. It appeals to a lot of people in Scotland, and if you'll take my advice, you'll join the party now – and don't forget, the holder of the lucky membership card number drawn out of the bonnet by Billy Wolfe with his eyes shut facing both ways at the same time, could be MP for Moray and Nairn. Thank you.

Mrs Charlotte Square What a man! We will now rise and sing the party song – one, two, three . . . (*One sings 'Scots wha hae', another 'Scotland the Brave', and another 'Floor o' Scotland'.*)

After a short cacophony, a moment of confusion, they ALL *go, to taped screams, etc.* YOUNG HEN *comes on, furious.*

Young Hen Is that how you think we are?

Old Hen It's no' so far off . . . some of yous are a sight worse – –

Young Hen Aye, I know, I've got tae admit it – but some of us is a lot better – in my branch we want mair than freedom for Scotland – we want social justice.

Old Hen Social justice? What the hell kind of a Tory expression is that?

Young Hen Tory?

Old Hen How can you have social justice without economic justice? – and how can you have economic justice without socialism? You know fine what I'm sayin' . . .

Young Hen But some of us *are* socialists.

Old Hen Aye, so you say – but where *are* ye? Let's hear from you.

Young Hen The first thing we've got to do is get Scotland *free*, then you'll see where the socialists are.

Old Hen Do you no think that might be a wee bit late? Let's be hearing from you *now*, before your bankers and your think-tank and your failed Tories take you over completely.

Young Hen Aye, but first we must get independence, so we've got to stay united. After independence . . .

Old Hen Oh God. Here we go again – do you no see what I'm sayin' to you? Now come on – for it matters, girl: what are you gonnae dae any different from us? You're gonnae move your parliament from London to Edinburgh, but it's gonnae still be there tae keep the people quiet and under the thumb – what difference is any of that gonnae make? None at all. And your precious oil – look – there's not one man – or woman – in your party gonnae make that much impact on the multinational corporations – all you'd be gettin' after independence is a few people grabbin' a bigger slice of the same bloody capitalist cake – Come on, girl – I'm waiting for you tae speak.

Young Hen Aye, well, I cannae get a word in edgeways – –

Old Hen Well try to avoid stupid expressions like social justice – you lot don't *read* enough, you use words that don't mean anythin'. You've learnt nothin' from two hundred years of working-class history. All you can do is – Scotland! Well, don't forget, *I'm* for a free Scotland: free of England, aye, but free of capitalist greed, misery and exploitation – right. Go.

Young Hen Well. I don't know. It's just we stand mair chance on our own . . .

Old Hen True, true.

Young Hen And we believe in democracy – I know that – and participation.

Old Hen Participation? What's that mean? Put the unions on the board wi' the bosses? An old capitalist trick tae con the workers – nothing more nor less – –

Young Hen Gran, can I finish?

Old Hen Aye, but you'll need to do better than that.

Young Hen Ah, hell, Gran – can you no see – it's an emotional thing – it's pride, the pride of a whole nation that wants to be free.

Old Hen Aye, I know . . . I feel it myself – But, but, *but*.

Young Hen And Scotland's on the move – right now.

Old Hen And so were we – but do you no' see the mistake we made: we put politics – that's Westminster and government, up here, and it failed us. Then we put economics – that's unions and General Strikes and abolition of capitalism, up here – and it failed us: why? Because the two must go together. When the working-class of Scotland gets itself on the move, and organised, for both together – *then* you'll see something. That's what you should be fighting for.

Young Hen I'll need tae think about that – –

Old Hen So you will. Here, I'm away now, to get these pamphlets out – imagine that lad in prison still for defending his pals against MacAlpine's thugs. (*Gives her a pamphlet.*) Here, it's just like nineteen twenty-six all over again – now come in and see me when you can – don't forget – I enjoy a wee blether with you, girl. It's true, she's a good girl: Cheery-bye now. (*Goes.*)

YOUNG HEN *looks at pamphlet then looks up wondering.* OTHERS *come on as themselves, repeating lines they have acted before.*

Mother Alright, so when wee Agnes died, me and your father moved in here and Henrietta on the floor and you got the room to yourself – bloody lucky you were, too . . .

Father Meetin', votin'? Here, don't waste your good pamphlets on me: I don't vote, nor do I go to meetin's . . .

George I'm fed up being a working-class fool.

Charlie You'll no get anything without a bit of trouble, Freddie.

KING GEORGE V *appears at the back of the stage in his robes.*

King George V We suppose we might as well let them play at being Prime Ministers and Home Secretaries and that sort of thing. As far as we can see it won't make any difference to anything serious: our City owns all our money. Our industrialists own our industries, our Church owns the minds of our people – we have our Army, our Navy, our Air Force and our police constables to see to that. (*Goes.*)

Maxton I could ask no greater job in life than to make English-ridden, capitalist-ridden, landowner-ridden Scotland into the Scottish Socialist Commonwealth – and in doing that, I'd be doing a great service to the people of England, Wales and the world.

Gallacher I believe there is only one way for the working people of this country to end the exploitation of their labour and their lives, and that is to seize state power, retain it, and establish the dictatorship of the proletariat as a means of transition to a communist society.

Wheatley At the present moment workers' representatives are powerless in the House of Commons. All our eggs must not be found in the parliamentary basket.

Maxton In the end you find you have built not the Palace of Socialist Freedom, but a slum dwelling for the working-class.

Maclean The day of social pottering or reform is past. However Labour may attain power, it must get full possession of the land and all means of production in order to use these co-operatively by the whole community for the benefit of all.

Singer (*Sings*) Little Hen gives all her strength to win that fight,
Seems her strength is never done;
Little Hen gives all she has, she knows she's right –
Nothing's going to stop her, till the fight is won.

Beat of MUSIC *changes.* LIGHTS *change.* SINGER *turns to audience. The rest of* COMPANY *join in as the last song progresses:*

You working folk of Scotland,
All you who want her free
Remember John Maclean right well
Or free you'll never be

What freedom you call
Is not freedom at all
Till tyranny is done
Not England alone but the tyrants at home
Must go before we've won.

What good's your flags and banners
What good's your Bannockburn
When Scotland's full of money-men
Who'll rob you in their turn

What freedom you call, etc.

We'll proudly build a Scotland
Where landlords' fences fall
Whose industry's for you and me
Where each can work for all

What freedom you call, etc.

You working folk of Scotland
All you who want her free
Remember John Maclean right well
Or free you'll never be.

At end of last song, BLACK-OUT.

END OF PLAY

Playscripts

available from
Pluto Press
Unit 10 Spencer Court, 7 Chalcot Road,
London NW1 8LH

Complete list of
Pluto books and pamphlets
available on request

John McGrath

Fish In The Sea

Liverpool in the 1970s. Into the complicated texture of the family life of the Maconochies, two powerful forces erupt. One is the occupation of the factory where Mr Maconochie earns his living: a determined, patient, organised working-class action against the ruthless rationalisation of a multi-national corporation. The other is the arrival of Andy, a Glaswegian wild man – anarchist, individualist, articulate – who recognises in Mary, one of the daughters, a kindred spirit.

Written for the Everyman Theatre, Liverpool, it broke all box-office records there during its run. Presented later by 7:84 Theatre Company, with music for its many songs by Mark Brown, it received great acclaim from critics and public in London, and played to enthusiastic working-class audiences all over England and Wales.

'has much of the dramatic skill, powers of invention and insight into character for which McGrath is justly renowned . . . The characterisations and relationships are superbly drawn. The Maconochie family are entirely believable, both individually and collectively . . . and there are many funny, sad and memorable scenes.' *Plays and Players*

'The author of *Fish In The Sea* is John McGrath, a generous, humorous writer, and a realist in the best sense of the word.' *New Statesman*

'it is difficult to do full justice to the play's richness' *Guardian*

'the characters are drawn with . . . sympathy and with . . . a fine ear for different speech idioms' *The Times*

John McGrath

The Cheviot, the Stag and the Black, Black Oil

The Highlands of Scotland – Euro-tourist paradise, haunt of grouse, deer and millionaire sportsman, famed for romantic song and majestic scenery – is also the home of a unique people, a culture, a language, a way of life.

This play tells the story of that people, from the time they were cleared from their homes to make way for sheep in the first half of the nineteenth century, to today. It shows the clearances as more than just the ruthless greed of a few men, but as an inevitable part of a process that is still going on in the operations of the oil giants and the multi-nationals.

It takes the form of a Highland *ceilidh* – a mixture of songs, jokes, sketches, music and narrative – to tell the tale.

Distributed by Pluto Press